T0354854

SUCCESSION

A Novel

SALVATORE MAMONE

SUCCESSION
A NOVEL

iUniverse books may be ordered through booksellers or by contacting:

iUniverse
1663 Liberty Drive
Bloomington, IN 47403
www.iuniverse.com
844-349-9409

ISBN: 978-1-6632-6379-7 (sc)
ISBN: 978-1-6632-6380-3 (e)

Library of Congress Control Number: 2024911806

Print information available on the last page.

iUniverse rev. date: 06/13/2024

This book is dedicated to my brother Vincent who lived through all the years of my life both good and bad and now at my end time my constant companion.

I acknowledge the assistance of the following people for their help in reviewing and editing this book and made it a better document for the readers.

Doreen Mamone
Louis Mamone
Vincent Mamone

PROLOGUE

My name is Mark Wu. You may not know me but you know John Water alias Peter Marks. I have been fortunate to come into possession of his logs and papers which give some insight of his life but can never explain or excuse why he did, what he did other than to say that he was evil.

There are people who are evil but there are very few people who are born evil. John was born evil and when he was assaulted when he was very young, he became more so. Most of the things that he did are in the papers and on TV but this document will tell you more. You will learn what he did but not always why. You will learn about his wife and how she dealt with him. You will learn about the people who tried to catch him before he commits the final murder, and you will find out how he was stopped and at what cost.

PART 1

John Water

CHAPTER 1

Killing is easy. I killed for the first time when I was seven. Now I will kill the President of the United States; and I can do it because I am the Vice-President.

CHAPTER 2

John was watching Michelle very carefully. He always watched everyone carefully. He had to; they were always after him. Everyone, especially Michelle. She was almost one year older than him; eight and she was John's biggest rival. John was in competition for everything; he had to be the best no matter what he did. He was going to get the best grades, get into the best schools, and get the best job; and no one was going to get in his way; certainly not Michelle.

To John, Michelle was this little bug that was just a little better than him in school and she had to be swashed. Who was she to be better? Who asked her to be better? Why did she have to be better? She would not stand in his way. John would make sure of that. Today.

The town picnic, called the Black Cherry Festival, was going strong and most people had more food than they should or could handle. Now the annual softball game was starting and those who could still walk were getting their gloves ready. Some of the men could barely walk but they still wanted to make a fool of themselves on the field. John could see fat "Uncle" Jack struggling to put on his glove. "Uncle" Jack was at least 150 pounds over weight but he still waddled over to the outfield. He was one of five outfielders so he could not make too many errors. Women were not allowed on the field, but then it was 1946. Women did not play sports in 1946. As far as John was concerned they should not play sports. They should do nothing but cook and clean, and take care of the family, like his mother. That is all they were good for; although later in life John would find that they were good for something else. Some of them.

There were so many people on the field that it would be almost impossible to get a hit. But that also made it easy for John because no one would be looking at him.

John was watching Michelle very carefully now. With the game getting started he had his chance to get rid of his main competition in life. John knew that Michelle was not interested in baseball; she was a bird watcher. Of course she was; just like a girl. Michelle walked down the trail and then off the trail in the hope of watching a new bird with her old worn binoculars. She was carrying her bird manual in one hand and the binoculars in another. She was so intent in what she was doing that she would never hear or notice John and John was far enough away that no one would notice or remember that he and Michelle were together.

There was a large lake just a short walk from the blind that Michelle was using. If she moved just 50 feet to the left he would have his chance; and then she did. John wore his old Keds and they were his favorite because people could not hear him sneak up on them. John liked to sneak up on people and scare the daylights out of them. Most times they would throw their hands in the air and scream. He loved to hear them scream. Once, "Uncle" Jack had actually peed in his pants when John scared him. John could still see the stain on Jack's pants and hear people laugh at the joke and at Jack. That was a good day. Today would be better.

Slowly John circled Michelle until he was right behind her; the little angel. Well, after today she would be a real angel. She was so interested in some bird, a bird that she had probably seen a dozen times, that she never heard him but she did feel the breeze when John swung and hit her with a large black rock. After that she could not hear or see anything. Life was over for her but going strong for John.

Now John had to get rid of the body, but he had already come up with a plan. He could always be counted on to come up with a plan. He would get rid of the body but in such a way that it would be found. He would dump her body in the lake.

Although John was big for his age he still had trouble moving Michelle to the lake. He had to carry her most of the way because he did not want to leave any drag marks. When he was finally at the lake he pushed her into the cold calm water. He quickly threw the rock as far as he could and then cleaned up the area of any blood. No one would suspect a seven year old boy of murder. Why, with any luck they would think that she fell into the lake and hit her head. The poor little thing.

Good riddance.

John walked back to the picnic area, not too fast but fast enough that he would not be missed or noticed. When he got back to his mother's table he noticed that the game was still going on. Even though it was an hour after he followed Michelle, no one had noticed Michelle was missing. John had quietly come back and was now sitting on the sidelines watching the adults making fools of themselves; something that he knew that he would never do.

"Look at the fools", he thought, "Running around getting sweaty, falling down, laughing; and no one has noticed someone is missing."

But as it started to get dark and people began to clean their tables someone finally asked about Michelle.

"Michael, have you seen Michelle?" Pam asked her husband.

"No I haven't; maybe she is looking for birds. She did bring her binoculars and bird book with her."

"Well it is late, see if you can find her."

"OK", Michael said.

John watched as Michael started down the trail to the lake. This was the same trail that Michelle often took and Michael expected to find her nearby. After searching for a while and calling for Michelle Michael began to realize that something was wrong. That is when he ran back to the picnic and asked for help. After a frantic hour of searching everyone was becoming very upset and someone finally decided to call the police for help. That did not make John happy. He knew the police would find her.

The police came quickly, too quickly for John, and with the bright external lights on their cruisers they still could not find her. With all the people looking for Michelle, footprints were all over the place. John was quick to realize this could be good for him. With all the foot traffic any evidence would be lost. After another hour of fruitless searches someone decided to get a boat and check the lake. And that is when they found her.

When she was pulled from the lake she had not started to turn colors and become bloated yet; but if she had stayed in the water a few hours more she would have. Now people began to scream and one woman actually fainted. John liked that. A lot.

Michael jumped in the water and helped bring his daughter to shore and then he had to help support his wife. She was inconsolable. The aunts and uncles and other relatives of Michelle were now gathered around and the crying was becoming unbearable to John. Although he was glad Michelle was gone he still had just a glimmer of grief. He was just seven and he did not understand the finality of death but he did know that Michelle was gone and it was his fault. It would not be the only time he would cause someone to die, but it was the only time that he felt any grief.

The police covered Michelle's body with a large blanket that they had in their car and put her in an ambulance. Her parents went with Michelle in the ambulance and several aunts and uncles and friends followed in their own cars. Because John and his mother were not relatives they just went home. John's mother, Rachael, was crying too; not because she knew Michelle well but because Michelle was just a child. She could not understand how God could take such a young child. Little did she know that it wasn't God but the devil reborn that took Michelle; fortunately she never found out.

This was John's first murder and for sure not his last. Later, at home, John felt very little of anything. He did extra homework for the extra credit he hoped to get and then he went to bed. He did not even have any nightmares. John was able to sleep the sleep of innocents except he was not innocent. The only time that he was ever innocent was when he was still in his crib and that did not last long. John was a bad seed and would always be a bad seed. There was no known reason why he would be this way; it just was the way he developed. Somehow or somewhere something happen that caused him to be the evil person that he was and would become. Whatever it was would remain unknown forever. His mother never saw the evil in her son, to her he was her "little man"; someone who would rise to great things; and he would; but not in the way that she imagined.

It took several days before the autopsy was completed and the body was ready before the funeral could be held. Although the condition of Michelle's body was not bad, she had a closed coffin funeral. Her parents could not bear to see her dead. The autopsy report was conclusive because Michelle had water in her lungs and therefore the cause of dead was listed as drowning. If the forensics that we have today were available in 1946, the coroner could have probably verified that she was murdered. But with the limited tests that were available and that he performed; the best the coroner could say was that Michelle fell in the water, hit her head and drowned.

After a two day funeral that was surreal in the amount of crying, Michelle was finally buried. None of the plans that her family had for her would ever be realized and she would never leave the town where she was born. But John would. And when he left; fortunately for the town, he would never return.

CHAPTER 3

Kevin Lightfeather was a Native American who was a proud member of the Iroquois League. The Iroquois League consisted of five original Indian nations with a six added later. He belonged to the Seneca Nation; which was the furthest West member of the league. He could remember the many tales that his grandfather and others talked about the Iroquois League and the Seneca Nation. Since the Iroquois had no official writing system the only way that the history and traditions of the Iroquois could be passed on was through the spoken word and through wampum belts. Kevin had never seen an original wampum belt but he had seen several duplicates and they were beautiful. The belts told stories about the people and could be translated by the elders. The original belts were stored at Onondaga, the capital of the Iroquois confederacy. Kevin had been told that the Iroquois had such a good formal method of government that some famous early American politicians, such as Thomas Jefferson and Ben Franklin, were closely involved with the Iroquois. Some historians believe that the Iroquois Constitution had influence in the American constitution. Kevin did not know if that was true or not but Kevin had a lot to be proud of as a member of the Iroquois confederacy. He owed his first name to the fact that many of the league used Christian names after being converted by the missionaries. His family; however, kept the last name because they wanted him to remember his heritage. And he always would.

Although there were still many Iroquois living in Canada, his family came from New York State near Lake Erie. They were poor, as were many Indians and other non-Indians, but they did the best that they could for their son. Even though Kevin was young everyone could tell that he was smart and everyone knew that he had a future ahead of him. He could be anything that he wanted to be; and one day he would make the family and the tribe proud.

Kevin and his family lived on the Allegany Indian reservation in a city called Salamanca. Salamanca is the only city in the United States that lies completely on an Indian Reservation. Kevin enjoyed living in Salamanca because he could learn from his tribe and from the non-Indians in town. His days were filled with chores and listening to his grandfather as he told stories about the old days. While he was still young and not yet in school, he helped gather the "three sisters" that the tribe still ate as a big part of their diet. This combination of corn, beans and squash was a reason why many of the tribe, and he, were healthy. There were still some horses on the reservation and Kevin learned to ride at an early age. There were others on the reservation that could ride and knew the Indian ways better than Kevin, but he was learning fast. He wanted to be a good Indian, a good member of the tribe, and a good student. When school started next year, he would be on his way to mastering all three.

Many people mistakenly believe that the Seneca live in huts or teepees, but that was not true certainly not in the 1950's. Most lived in houses and some lived in apartments in town. They were poor but so were many other people they knew. They considered themselves a large family and in many ways they were. The members of the tribe took care and looked out for each other whether they belong to the same family or not. Most people belonged to these extended families.

Kevin's grandfather, named Joseph Charles but nicknamed JC, was a robust man with a stern appearance, but a mild temperament. He had a weather-beaten face, as did most elderly Seneca's, and a long regal nose. When he stood up to his full 6'3" frame he was an imposing sight. JC loved children and children loved him in return. He could always be found with some small children by his side, either his grandchildren or his neighbors. Kevin, the son of his daughter, was a favorite of JC. He took Kevin everywhere and taught him everything. He taught him to fish and hunt. He taught him how to ride a horse and how to drive a car. He taught him to enjoy life and he taught him to be kind to everyone. Kevin's temperament was a gift from JC. Many times during long walks JC would tell Kevin about the old days and how badly the tribe was treated and how many treaties the government broke when it was convenient. He told Kevin about the Nation's representative government known as the Grand Council. The Grand Council is the oldest governmental institution still maintaining its original form in North America. Each tribe sends chiefs to act as representatives and make decisions for the whole nation. The Seneca tribe sent 8 chiefs. He told Kevin that their clan was the bear clan and was much respected in the tribe. He told Kevin many other things about the tribe and the ways of the tribe and he told Kevin that he could tell that one day Kevin would be destined for good things. Kevin loved JC and he wanted his grandfather's belief in Kevin to materialize. With hard work, it would.

CHAPTER 4

John hated everyone in school; the students, teachers, he even hated the white rats in their little glass cage. All they did all day was eat, sleep, run around in circles, and shit. What an easy life they had.

John was in 4th grade now and he was getting smarter and meaner. He had no friends and that was fine with him. Who had time for friends? He had too much to learn and do. He had heard that he would be skipping 5th grade soon because there was nothing for him to learn in 4th grade; he was quickly outgrowing the school. He had hoped that he would have skipped the 6th grade too but that would come soon enough. Little by little he was growing to his full potential and soon everyone would know it.

His father, Martin, had left home when John was two and his mother was forced to care for him alone. His father leaving home was no loss because his father was usually drunk and unemployed. The little work that he could find barely put food on the table so when he left; neither John nor his mother wept. The few people that knew John's parents had no idea where Martin went; some said New York, others Phoenix, but once he left no one could remember ever seeing him again. John thought that his father was probably in some pauper's grave somewhere; with a cardboard coffin, and an unnamed marker in an unknown cemetery. John wanted more for himself and his mother.

John and his mother Rachael lived in a small town in Pennsylvania called Kane. Kane was a rural community that was near the Allegany National Forest. It was a small town, about 6,000 people, with the vast majority being white. Others had not yet discovered this interesting town. The winters in Kane were so cold that Kane was called the "Ice Box of Pennsylvania." John and Rachael lived in a small apartment, in a small town, in a large state. When winter came the cheap walls, poor installation, and drafty widows made living and sleeping in the apartment almost as bad as being outside, Rachael called it a "cold hell". Even a small, old, space heater, with worn wires did not help much. In the winter, when they went to sleep, they went to sleep wearing clothes and a coat. Their apartment was not much more than four walls and a place to hang their pitiful stack of clothes. But it was all they had and all Rachel would ever have. During spring the apartment was almost bearable. Rachael would bring in some wild flowers that grew in a local lot and the apartment looked almost livable. In summer the one window could be left open when someone was home and that took most of the heat out of the apartment but brought in the smells from a local restaurant; a restaurant that they did not have the money to use. In early fall they could see the trees change colors and see the small animals getting ready for the upcoming winter. And in winter all they could see was their breath.

Rachael did the best that she could with her main job as a secretary at the lumber mill and her second job working tables at a local dinner. She did not make much money and she was too tired when she returned home to care for John; but John did not need any help. He was fine alone. And at this point in his life he liked being alone. John would; however, remember how good his mother was to him and he was going to repay her for her hard work and kindness. When he had money he was going to make sure that he shared it with her no matter how much trouble it caused him. That was a silent vow that he would live to keep.

CHAPTER 5

Kevin's parents worked hard to send their only son to a "white man's" school in the hope that he would get into a good college one day. He would be the first one in his family to graduate from college and he would make his family and tribe proud. In order to ensure he get a good education they sent him to a small school in a town outside of the reservation. A sister of Kevin's mother, Cynthia, had an apartment and a job in Kane, a small town in northern Pennsylvania. The job didn't pay much and the apartment was small but she had a sofa bed that Kevin could use. The apartment overlooked one of the main streets in town and had wall to wall walls with only one window from which you could say that you had a view of a back road. The lack of windows made the apartment warm in summer but comfortable in winter. For all its shortcomings, Cynthia kept the apartment clean and the refrigerator full.

Cynthia was a small, pretty, dark, thirty-five-year-old woman who lost her husband, Marshall, in a bar fight. Too many people on the reservation ended up that way, but Cynthia's husband got into a bar fight in Kane. After one too many drinks, that he could not afford, on a night of one too many boosts and Marshall ended up as another statistic. After Marshall died Cynthia could have moved back to the reservation but she liked it in Kane. She had a good job in the local mill and she was treated well by the other people in the company. No one treated her different because she was a Seneca Indian, probably because she was not the only Seneca in town. She was hoping to make some money and maybe find a new husband in town. Pickings were slim but she could always hope. She still had her looks and she was a good woman and she still had dreams. Kevin was not part of those dreams but he was a good addition to her life.

The addition of Kevin gave her someone to talk to and gave her the "son" she never had with Marshall. For all Marshall's faults, and he had plenty, Cynthia could never say that he was bad in bed, but whether it was from all the horseback riding or some early injury, or chemicals from the mill, Marshall shot blanks and Cynthia never had the child that she wanted. Kevin would fill that void.

Kevin adjusted to the town and the people fast and he was eager to help Cynthia in any way he could. He helped with the cleaning and carrying the wash to the local laundry mart, and he even wanted to help with the cooking, which Cynthia was glad to oblige. Kevin was smart and studied every night and Cynthia could only marvel at what a good person her nephew was and how much better he was becoming. Her sister and her sister's husband did a good job with Kevin and Kevin would definitely become an asset to the family and the tribe. Although Kevin was very young and just starting school he told everyone that he wanted to be a lawyer, and people knew that he would make it. Everyone knew that Kevin would be anything that he wanted to be and he would not windup like Marshall.

CHAPTER 6

It was finally Friday of another long boring week and as usual John did not learn much in class. The teachers could not teach him anything because he knew almost as much as they did.

"What a waste of time," he thought.

"I could learn just as much on my own."

There is no excitement at school and John wanted excitement. What could he do that would be fun. And then he knew.

"The rats! Of course." said John.

That afternoon at lunch when everyone was eating or playing games, John snuck back into class and when no one was looking he opened the cages and twisted the necks of each rat until they were dead. They made just the slightest noise when they died.

"Oh what a fun week this has been," he said.

"Wait until the kids see what happened, they will be surprised."

It wasn't until 2pm when one of the kids, Peter was his name, said, "What is wrong with the mice?"

The teacher, an old wrinkled used up hag named Susan, slowly limped over to the cages on her one good leg and let out a loud gasp. One look told her the rats were dead.

"What happened to the mice?" she said.

"Did any one notice what happened"?

"No" the class said in unisons: was it something they ate?" someone said.

Susan could not be sure but with all her experience teaching and being around kids she just knew that John had something to do with the death of the rats. She could smell how mean he was. He actually gave off an odor that said "Bad", and she could smell it. After all her years as a teacher she had a second sense about the kids. She knew which ones would grow up to be good citizens and which would not and John would definitely not be a good citizen. She actually hoped that he would not grow up because she was afraid of what he would do as an adult. She was afraid of what he could do now. She could not wait until he left her class, her school, her city and her state. She did not want to be within a thousand miles of him. In all of her years as a teacher she never felt this way about a student before.

Susan could not prove that John killed the rats so all she could do was remove the rats from their cage and dispose of them. Some of the children, mostly girls, were crying.

"What happened to the mice?" they cried.

But Susan did not know and so all she could say was, "I don't know".

She wanted to let the kids out early but there was no way to get them home so she used the rest of the day consoling those children that took it the hardest. Of course, John was smiling as if he did not have a care in the world, and as a matter of fact; he didn't. Later that day, after class was let out, Susan examined the rats more thoroughly and when she picked up the mice she could see that something was wrong with their necks. She knew then what John had done.

"That boy is evil." "He is the evilest person I have ever met." "God give me strength to get through this year."

And Susan's prayers were answered. To Susan's great delight John was transferred to the fifth grade were he would be another teacher's problem. And he was.

CHAPTER 7

As John expected, fifth grade was no challenge.

"When will they teach me something that I don't already know?" he wondered. "When will they teach me something that I need to know?" he questioned. The only thing that happened in the fifth grade was that John began to notice the girls. He never paid much notice of the girls before; he never paid much notice to anyone before; but for some reason the girls in the fifth grade looked different. They were taller, some were starting to get small bumps, and he was attracted to them and he did not know why. There was no way that he could do anything physical with them even if he knew what to do but he liked looking at them and they were becoming a distraction; a distraction that he did not need.

As usual, John did not have any friends in class; he just could not relate to the other students. None of the students seemed to have the same needs, ideas, or knowledge that John had. John was competitive but he did not have anyone to compete with. This was good and bad; good because it helped John relax; as much as he could ever relax, bad because he didn't have anyone to push him. He wanted to be pushed and pushed hard. The teacher did not know what to do with him. He was the smartest student she had ever seen but his reputation told her that he was also the meanest student she would ever see. There was no "genius" class in those days, teachers taught to the average student, so John had to find things to do or he would become totally bored. Often times John would have crazy or dangerous ideas and then carry them out. One time John saved his "droppings", put them in several bags and left the bags where others would step in them. When that happened, John laughed so hard that milk came out of his nose. Another time, just for fun, John "refilled" the library cards in a new order that he thought up. He could always come up with new ways to keep busy and to be as happy as someone like him could be.

John used his time to read every book in the small school library that he could find. He would ask his mother for money to buy more books but with her limited income that was almost always impossible. Once in a while she could indulge his needs but not often. John did not hold that against her; he knew how hard it was for her, but he needed an outlet for his boredom. And that outlet was called Kevin.

There was one strange boy in class; strange to everyone in class. He was a Native American that went by the name of Kevin Lightfeather. He belonged to the Iroquois confederacy and just his appearance was interesting. He transferred to the school from the reservation and was now a member of John's fifth grade.

Kevin dressed just like the rest of the boys in class but he looked very different. For one thing he was dark, for another he had the longest, the darkest and the straightest hair that anyone had ever seen. He was also the tallest and handsomest boy in class, even more so than John. He would need to beat the girls off with a stick in a couple of years and based on how tall he was, he had the stick.

John was very interested in Kevin because he was always interested in the unusual. John had read about Indians in his school text and in other books, but this was the first Indian he had ever gotten close to. John wanted to learn all he could about Kevin's tribe and this at last gave him something exciting to do. John needed to get to know Kevin but John was smart enough that he knew not to antagonize Kevin because John knew that even though Kevin was quiet and soft spoken, Kevin could crush him. John needed to be quiet around Kevin and not make any waves.

Once in a while John made conversation with Kevin, just to see what Kevin though and what he believed. John and Kevin were not what anyone would call friends, but for John this was as close to a friend as you could get. John watched how the girls in class made funny goofy faces when Kevin was around. John had never seen girls act like that before and he could not understand what it meant. Although Kevin was a year older

19

than John, he was much smarter in the ways of "the birds and the bees" than John. Most people that live on farms or reservations know about sex because they see what the animals do.

Kevin was not immune to what his good looks caused girls to do. Whenever Kevin's family visited for the yearly large family get-togethers, he watched how the older boys and girls acted. He also noticed how the young girls looked at him. They would giggle and laugh and talk about him. He would be very popular in a few years. With his exotic looks and his intelligence he could be anything that he wanted to be, and he still wanted to be a lawyer. He wanted to work for the tribe and help the Indians recover some of the land that was stolen from them. Most of the treaties that were signed with the government only favored the government and even with the treaties in the governments favor, the government still disregarded the treaties when it was to their benefit. Kevin wanted to make the U.S. Government stand by those treaties. He knew that it would be a hard road to travel and he knew that his family did not have much money, but he also knew that he would do it.

John and Kevin made a strange pair; both were smart and handsome but in all other regards they could not be further from each other. John was an introvert and so was Kevin but Kevin was slightly more out-going. John was mean and Kevin was kind to everyone. John was smart because his brain was wired that way, while Kevin had to apply himself and work hard for his grades. They talked to each other, but they could never be friends. Both had high expectation but only one, Kevin, wanted to use his talents for good. John spoke to Kevin to learn and to learn how to use Kevin. Kevin spoke to John because Kevin was curious about all the rumors he had heard. Could John actually be as bad as he had heard? Each had a use for each other but neither had a like for the other.

They would usually speak at lunch or whenever there was a break from class. John would question Kevin on his tribe, what were they like, did they live in teepees (no), why was his hair so long (tradition), can he ride a horse (yes), John asked Kevin everything he could think of. Kevin answered in a soft even tone, but he seldom asked any questions of John. Kevin could tell what John was like just by looking at him. The more Kevin looked and listened to John, the more he knew that the stories he had heard were true. John would be a good person to watch and to avoid.

Eventually John could not think of any more questions to ask and he grew tired of Kevin, John could not gain anything else from Kevin, so they both just drifted away. They were in the same class but they were not in the same class.

CHAPTER 8

Portia Marshall was a beautiful young woman from a good family from the best part of Philadelphia. She had everything going for her, especially her ability to twist the boys around her manicured fingers. All the boys in class and town were after her and none could have her. She knew what she was and what she had and she was enjoying her skill in making the boys and men twist and turn and have wet dreams. She was only in seventh grade but she looked older. When men and boys looked at her, they drooled and only thought of one thing, "How can I get her in bed?" The answer was simple, "Keep dreaming." she thought. She would only have sex when she was ready to and with whom she wanted, and so far, no one she knew met that second criteria. She would keep the boys twisting and drooling and she enjoyed ever minute of it.

Her house (she liked to call it *her* house) was more a mansion than a house. It had three levels with multiple fireplaces; more bathrooms than could be used; a large three-bedroom guesthouse; and was situated on 12 prime acres just outside of Philadelphia. Portia's bedroom was almost as large as some apartments, but that was fitting since she was an only child. The furniture in her room was French and very expensive with a canopy bed that would make Marie Antoinette proud. Her father pampered her and gave her anything she wanted and she wanted a lot. But she was reasonable with her requests. She could have the most expensive clothes and jewels but she was not ostentatious. She was so beautiful that jewels could distract from her natural beauty. She was the princess in the family and she always would be and she knew it.

Portia got her looks from her mother and it was a good thing because her father, although a wonderful man, was not handsome. He was tall, as was her mother, and slim, especially for his age. He still had most of his hair but it had started to turn white. He was of medium complexion and still had all his teeth. He wore glasses but only to read and he was still athletic. Her father, Edward, was in real estate and although he inherited money on his mother's side, with smarts and luck Edward vastly increased the family fortune. The family had more money than they could ever use and as their only child, Portia, stood to inherit it all. The question on her family's mind was therefore, make sure she marries well. That meant someone with a good future and with his own money; poor need not apply. If he was handsome, as her family expected, then they would probably produce handsome grandchildren.

Portia would have everything that anyone could want and she would be the best catch in Philadelphia and maybe even on the East coast. Her father took her to all the right places to meet the right people and eventually, when she became older and graduated from college, he would bring her into the family business. Although she was as smart as she was beautiful, she was smart enough to hide her intelligence. She had the one important trait that she needed to be successful, she was cunning and she knew to talk only when necessary. This made her appear to be a "dumb blonde" but her father was the only person that knew how smart and cunning she was and he knew that she would one day be able to take over the family fortune. She would be one of the few female head of a large company.

Portia, of course, could not go to just any school; she needed a preparatory academy to ensure that she would get into the best college. The school that she would attend was small and had an enrollment of fewer than 300. The teacher to student ratio was one teacher to seven students, which ensured special tutoring. The tuition was more than most people pay for a good college, but Edward knew what he wanted for his only child; he wanted the best; and Queen Ann Preparatory was the best. The fact that Edward was a prime contributor to the school made it easy for Portia to gain admission to this very exclusive and restrictive school. The fact that Portia would be one of the best students ever to attend Queen

Ann's made her admission a given. She would spend the four years learning the normal courses, plus she would attend classes on etiquette and social skills. Portia would need the social skills because both she and Edward had high hopes for her. She would marry well and rich and she would give Edward the grandchildren that he longed for. Edward was a good man and was a good father and nothing would make him happier than to play with his healthy, happy grandchildren. That would have to wait of course until Portia finished school and came out at the debutant ball; but Edward could wait. He had good genes and was in good health so he knew that time was on his side.

Edward had his life and his family's life planned out to the smallest detail. Attention to detail is how he made his fortune and how he ran his life. Attention to detail is what he would use to make a happy and rich life for his only child. He would make sure that nothing bad or evil would enter his beautiful daughter's life. But it would.

CHAPTER 9

John's life at school was progressing about as he expected – good grades, no friends. Life at home was not going as well as he hoped. His mother was still working multiple jobs; any extra job she could find, and she was getting older by the day. Each work day of 18 hours aged her two days. Her hair, the little she still had, was prematurely white and the skin on her face was worn, wrinkled, and dry. She was never a head-turner or even good looking; but now she was old and sickly and not pleasant to look at. John was only in the sixth grade and it was impossible for him to get a job, but as soon as he could legally or illegally work, he would. He needed to somehow get money to help his mother, the only person that mattered to him.

John had not skipped another grade as he expected and wanted. The school principal and the teachers knew that he was smart enough to skip a grade but they had never taught someone this smart and potentially evil before. If he skipped a grade, he could also be two years younger than anyone else in class. Because the other students were experiencing puberty, he would definitely be confused and out of place. John knew that if he continued to get the grades that he always managed to get that the school had to let him skip another grade. He would be completely out of place if he didn't skip a grade; there was just nothing for him to learn. Also, the faculty was afraid of what he would do if he didn't skip a grade next year; they were afraid that he could really snap. He would not be old enough to be in the same grade as older teenagers but there was no way he could not skip another grade. Another problem that the teaching staff had to content with was; if John continued to skip grades, he would eventually be the youngest person in high school and college; how would he adjust?

Unlike most boys John's age, John did not play games, or run around with other boys his age. He was not interested in games and none of the other boys wanted to play with John or rather their parents would not let them play with John. It was almost as if John had a disease that people felt their kids would catch, like the flu; but what John had was not catching. What John had was terminal evil.

John's childhood was lonely and was probably a reason why his personality did not change and might be a reason that he became more interested in violence. He never met a small animal that he didn't kick or worse. He wore a smile but the smile did not fool anyone. He would never be able to hide what he really was or could be.

John did not see much of Kevin anymore especially since Kevin was in a higher grade. One strange thing; however, had happened this year; John was beginning to notice the girls in class, especially the ones with small chest bumps. The girls had not noticed John for two reasons: one, John was too young, and two, because of his reputation. John was not at all interested in his reputation but so far this school year he did not cause any trouble that could be traced back to him. There was the incident of the small fire in the boy's bath room but for once it was not John that started the fire; not that anyone believed it. John was so concerned with his mother's health that he did not have time for mischief in school. He still would get the highest grades in his class, even when he didn't study, but that did not remove the reputation that followed him and would follow him until a few years later when he didn't change but his life would.

CHAPTER 10

John wondered what he was doing. He had not had sex yet but he wanted to learn and he felt that 14 was a good age to start. What better way than to learn from a pro. One of the boys in school mentioned a place where he "did the dirty" and John felt that this was his chance to learn. John took the local bus to a run-down part of town and found the building and room that he was told to visit. John had never been to this part of town and he knew that he looked out of place. A young white boy with clean clothes and a new haircut probably did not live around here. If anyone saw him, they had to figure that he was only here for one of two reasons, drugs or sex or both.

John walked up two flights and came to the apartment that he was told about. Based on the condition of the walls in the apartment building John was having second and third thoughts about what he was doing. John waited a moment, still afraid, but not scared, and then he knocked. A voice from the other side answered.

"Who is it?"

John then gave the "call sign", "A friend" he answered.

After a few very nervous seconds a middle-aged woman with obvious bleached hair answered the door. She was at least as old as his mother and not nearly as pretty. Her clothes were old and dirty and so was she. She had all her teeth but they looked like they had not made an appointment with a toothbrush in weeks. The room had a bed with sheets that should have been cleaned and then burned; the floor was littered with food droppings and the one light bulb in the room had more dust and dirt on it than his entire apartment. Now John really wanted to know what he was doing here. But then John remembered what someone had said, "You can always put a bag over her head." So, John decided to fantasize about being with someone else and take his mind off what was in front of him. Someone told him once that the main reason why people make love in the dark is so that they can fantasize about being with someone else and now he believed it. John thought about Connie in his class. Connie was tall with blond hair and every boy in class had wet dreams about her. If he was going to fantasize, she was a good choice.

"What's your name big boy?" she asked.

"My name is John but you can call me John." he said nervously. "What is your name?"

"My name is Michelle and you can call me anything you want. Do you want to have some fun?"

"The real question is; do *you* want to have some fun?"

"I like a man with confidence. I guess you are not new at this." Michelle said.

John lied and said "No I know what I am doing."

When Michelle saw his size 13 shoe she was very impressed because she could guess what else was that size. Michelle then answered, "Then let's see what you have."

And John did. He was amazed how fast he could get hard and how big he was. When he self-gratified at home he got big but now he seemed to be even bigger. His organ was gorged. Michelle was very impressed.

"Well now I see I *am* going to have fun. Let's see what you can do with that. Do you want to be natural or do you want to use a condom?"

"Why don't you put one on me," John answered.

Michelle did as she was asked and then she quickly took off the little bit of clothes she wore. She did not want to waste time and have John lose his erection. Young kids could come fast and then have nothing left. She did not know that there was no way that would happen, but she would soon find out. When John put his enormous organ inside her she wanted to scream but she was too much of a pro for that; but John was right, she was having fun; she almost felt that she should pay him but that would never happen; she *was* too much of a pro. John could not believe what he was doing and the little satisfaction he was receiving; she was obviously enjoying this more than him. Is this all there is he thought. What is the big deal? It would take more time and more women before he could answer those questions.

When he was done John paid her what she asked for and quickly, very quickly, threw on his clothes. Before leaving he looked at himself in the room's one old dirty cracked mirror and he looked the worse for wear. His hair looked like a tossed salad and his clothes looked as dirty as he felt. If that was sex, he thought it was no big deal. I could get better satisfaction by myself.

On the way back home, John tried to get some beer but even though he was tall for his age he did not look eighteen. The idea that he could get laid but not buy beer struck him as crazy and funny. If he had been mad, he probably would have punched the cashier and taken the beer, but how could he be mad after having sex for the first time; even if it was lousy sex.

By the time he arrived home, his mother, Rachael, had already gone to bed. As usual she had worked a long day and she needed her rest for tomorrow. She worked six to seven days a week for so long that she did not know what day it was or what a day of rest was. Even when she took a day off, all she did was sleep. She had no life, no loves, no leisure and no money. The only thing she had was John and the only thing John had was her. She hoped that she would live long enough to see her son become successful, but she never did. She never saw what he would become and she was better for not knowing.

"They were very poor but other people were able to survive and even thrive even though they were poor. No, there was something in John's makeup that caused him to be this way and she could not afford the money to find out. As for her, she could not remember the last time she visited a doctor, and as a result, several years later, when she finally went to see a local doctor, it was too late.

When John was young Rachael still looked pretty but the long hours

29

were catching up with her. She wanted to meet someone, someone who could love her and help take care of her and John; but she was worried about what John would do. John wanted her for himself and he would never share. She heard stories and rumors about John, some so terrible that she could never believe them, but if they were true then she could never bring anyone home. So Rachael was doomed to a life alone with a son that loved her but no one else. It was a platonic love between mother and son but it was also more; it was a love of appreciation. John appreciated Rachael and Rachael appreciated John for that love. That love kept her from ever getting married again; and it kept John from ever loving any women as much as he loved Rachael. The only love that John would ever be able to give to any women was lust and sex. And for John, that was enough; and for the woman, it had to be enough.

CHAPTER 11

Kevin had lived in Kane for several years now and was getting taller, smarter, better looking, and better liked. During the summer break he would go home to visit his family for a few weeks, but he could not stay long because he needed to payback Cynthia for everything, she did for him. Kevin needed to work to help Cynthia pay for the rent and food. Cynthia was still working at the mill but all the years breathing in the dust and chemicals were taking a toll on her small lungs. She never smoked but she had the lungs of someone who smoked several packs a day. Kevin did not want to windup like that so instead of working at the mill he did odd jobs around town. He was very handy with machinery and he knew more than the local mechanics about cars. This gave him an opportunity to work in several garages during the summer and when school was out. He was friendly with everyone and that made it easy for him to get a good reputation around town. People knew that he was reliable, quiet, and a good worker. These were all good traits that would serve him well later in college and as a lawyer.

Kevin was tall, not just tall for his age, but tall. He was going to inherit more than JC's personality; he would inherit his height. Kevin had lots of friends in school, but he did not hang around with John anymore. John seemed to be absent a lot, a fact not lost on the teachers either; but John still managed to get the best grades in class. The teachers never complained about John's absences because they did not want to take a chance and question John because of his known reputation for evil. John did not blow-up when he did not get his way as some people might; John just got even; and when John got even it was unable to prove but always vicious. There was this one time when one of the teachers made the mistake of criticizing John for some small infraction. The teacher was new and did not know John's history; but he learned soon enough when he saw his car had been spray painted black (the car was naturally white) and had manure spread on all the windows and door handles. Of course, no one saw what had happened but it was clear that it must have been John. If the teacher had not been desperate for a job he would have quickly resigned; as it was, he kept far away from John and never criticized him again.

When Kevin was able to go back home, he would sit for hours with JC and talk about JC's early life on the reservation. JC would sit around a large table and many teenagers and younger children would listen to JC tell what they thought were tall tales but were not. Later, Kevin would take long walks with JC and talk about the history of his family and the tribe and about how the tribe was made up. JC told Kevin that the Seneca nations own name means "People of the Great Hill" and the Seneca were know as the "keepers of the Western Door" because they settled and lived the farthest west of all nations within the Iroquois League. He told Kevin about the discussion with the government who wanted to build a dam on the Seneca lands.

CHAPTER 12

Portia was growing tall. She was always tall for her age; both her mother and father were tall, so the recent growth spurt was not surprising. She attended the best high school/finishing school in the area and was receiving the best grades. Fortunately, it was an all-female school which kept interactions with boys to a minimum. Whenever she left the school campus every male would notice her. Chiropractors made good money off the neck spasms she caused by all the turned heads. Now that Portia was older her father used her at the office during the summer months when school was out. Portia would have liked to spend the summer in Europe like some of her friends but she also appreciated the faith her father had in her. Her work in the office included learning the books and operations of the firm. The main function of the company was to make money in real estate. This included buying property and land that could appreciate in just a few years. This property could be local, national, or international. This took a lot of research and Portia watched how the senior members of the staff calculated values and projected these values into the future. Her father must have hired the best people because they were seldom wrong. Portia watched and spoke little. She was smart enough that she could understand what the researchers were doing but she was not smart enough to know why. Her father gave her a small office, just large enough that people would know that she was management material and not a secretary. No one every asked her to get them coffee. She attended most meetings and sometimes even asked intelligent questions, which made her father proud. The more that Andrew saw of Portia at work the more that he knew that she would be able to take over the firm when he was gone; which he hoped would be a long time in the future.

Portia was also getting ready for her debutant ball; which would be in the fall. Edward would spare no expense to make this the most expensive and formal ball anyone had ever seen. The ball would be held in the Edward's mansion because there was no hotel that could compare to the Marshall estate. Edward hoped that Portia might become friends with the young men and maybe find someone to date and maybe marry one day. That's basically what the debutant ball was for, But this year Portia did not see anyone she want to date, but she had lots of time.

CHAPTER 13

John was moving up in the world, at least as far as school was concerned. He was a junior in high school and because of his grades he was taking college credit courses. As far as John was concerned, the sooner he could finish school the better. His mother was not well and John did not know where he would go if something happened to her. He had no relatives and no one to take him in. If something happened to his mother, he would need to find a job to pay the rent and eat; but who would hire such a young kid? John's only hope was that his mother could last until he finished high school and then he could go to college. He knew that he could get a job in college. If that did not work out John could not think of any alternatives; except one and that one was dangerous.

Drugs were becoming bigger and bigger in town and in school. He had heard that some people could make good money dealing, but only if you were a high-level dealer; and that took time. He could try holdups but that was very dangerous; most robbers were caught. The one option that he could see involved this redneck in class named Howard Armstrong. What a stupid name for a redneck and a smuggler, John thought, but beggars and smugglers can't be choosey. Howard smuggled cigarettes and sometimes guns from the south to the north and he made good money on each run. If John could convince Howard to let him in on his side job that would allow him to make some money, enough that he could start saving. He was not concerned about the class he would miss because most of the runs were done on the weekends and John didn't need class anyway. This idea looked more and more possible and probable.

One day, after the last class of the day, John found Howard and began his approach to persuade Howard that John could be a big help in his after-school activities. One plus on John's side was the fact that Howard was interested in a small red head named Cindy. John knew Cindy but he was not really interested in her but she was interested in John. He liked taller women although once he got some more experience, he would not kick Cindy out of bed. Making Cindy aware of Howard's interest could be the deciding factor in John's favor. John might be.

Hello Howard," said John, "How are you doing?"

"Hello John, fair I guess." said Howard.

"I know that we don't talk much but I was wondering if you had a minute to talk with me now." "How are you and Cindy making out, or are you?"

"Well to tell you the truth John, I wish that she would give me the time of day. I have a right big crush on that sweet girl and I wish that I could get me some strength to talk to her."

God; how John hated to hear this redneck talk. It was almost like he had never taken an English class in his life. This was the big problem that John knew that he would have to face; could he bear to listen to that voice on a long drive and would he be able to talk like that as well. John was not sure that he had to talk like Howard but it might make it easier to be accepted.

"I was wondering about your after-school activities and whether I could get me a piece of the pie." questioned John.

"I could be a right help to you on those long drives. You do know that I know how to drive, right? Think about how much faster you can get the job done if I could drive."

"I don't know John; my suppliers may not like the idea."

"How about on your next run I go with you, for free of course, and you see how you like it and you can talk to your suppliers. I can also talk to Cindy for you, you know, smooth the way."

"Ok, but I can't tell you that the suppliers will agree."

"I understand, Howard, let me talk to them and see if I can convince them. As for Cindy, I don't know what Cindy will say but you never know. At least you might get your foot in the door; or better"

"That sounds right good to me John."

I've got to be able to convince Cindy to at least give Howard the time of day. The rest would be up to Howard. One day, after class, John saw his opening and began to reel in his prey.

"I will be meeting my supplier this weekend so why don't you all come with me as a trial run."

"That sounds good to me Howard. Let me talk to Cindy and I will get back to you."

John could sell ice to Eskimos but talking Cindy into going out with Howard would be a lot harder than that. Howard was medium height with dirty brown hair and eyes that were always open wide. He probably slept with his eyes open - like some wild animal. His clothes were out of date and always dirty although sometimes Howard was even dirtier. He drank a lot of Mountain Dew soda so his teeth (the ones he still had) were rotten. John would have to do a major selling job for Cindy to go out with Howard. After that, John needed to make the run this weekend and convince the suppliers that with two drivers they could make more than one run a week. If the supplier and distributor had any sense they would understand John's pitch. As for Cindy, one hand washes the other. Cindy could talk to Howard once and then let him down easy and John could do more than talk to Cindy and then let her down hard.

John had one more task to perform; Cindy had to talk to Howard. There was no time like the present so John searched and found Cindy at lunch and using his best voice tried to sell ice to Eskimos.

"Cindy, how are you?" said John.

"Hi John, I'm fine. You look good this morning."

"Thank you, Cindy, and so do you, as usual." John really had to pour it on thick.

"John I was wondering if you and I could go out some time. Maybe see a movie or something."

"Well thank you for asking Cindy but to be honest I have a small problem that maybe you could help me with."

"Sure John, how can I help?"

"You know Howard from class?"

"You mean that dirty boy that can't talk right?"

"That's him. He has a major crush on you and well, he asked me if I could talk you into talking to him."

"Are you kidding me? John, there is no way I would be seen dead with him."

"I understand completely. If I did not need him, I wouldn't even ask. All I'm asking is for you to say hi and speak to him one time. After that you can tell him in no uncertain terms that you are not interested. Five minutes that's all."

"I will make it up to you by taking you to a movie or whatever else you had in mind." John said.

With that John could see that Cindy's upper lip had little drops of water on it; she was starting to get interested. And hot.

"Why John, what kind of girl do you take me for?" Cindy said with a large smile on her face.

"I don't know Cindy; what kind of girl are you? Are you a good girl?"

"Yes" she replied.

"Are you a very good girl?" John asked.

"Yes." Cindy was now having trouble breathing.

"Would you like to try for fantastic?" John asked.

"Oh yes John I would." Cindy moaned.

"Why don't you talk to Howard tomorrow morning and then come and see me later. How does that sound?"

"Whatever you say John." said Cindy.

And that's how it happened. Cindy spoke to Howard for four minutes (she could not make it to five) and John did more than speak to Cindy - for an hour. And all three went away happy, some more than others.

CHAPTER 14

On Friday John and Howard left school after lunch and began the eight hour drive south. With John driving most of the way they made good time and never raised the interest of any cops on the highway. John read about all the tricks to avoid detection and they worked like a charm. Based on the way Howard drove it was a miracle that he had never gotten any tickets. With the goods they would be carrying back they definitely did not want to be stopped and searched. About 30 minutes early they arrived at the supplier and Howard started the conversation with a man that made Howard look and sound like a Princeton graduate.

"Howdy Howard; you looking fine."

"Thank you, kindly Moses, you looking good too."

Moses, John thought, some redneck named their son after a Jew? What did they think; the son would; part the sewers? John knew that he would need a long bath when he got back home; and not only because of the ride.

Moses looked like someone that did not believe the Civil War had ended, or if it did, the South had won. He wore a t-shirt with the rebel flag on it, he had several rifles within easy reach, and in case he needed assistance, two of the biggest, ugliest dogs John had ever seen. Both dogs looked like they were kicked and abused by Moses and that probably led to them being so mean. Both dogs looked like they ate small children for lunch and they would probably like one of John's arms for a snack. John kept as far away from the dogs as possible just in case the dogs did get hungry. And he stayed as far away from Moses as he could; in case John caught something from Moses; like ignorance.

"Moses, I want you to meet John; he came to help me on the drive."

"Howdy Moses, good to meet you." said John, reverting to redneck speak.

"And you John." "Now how is this going to work out?"

"Well I thought I could help with the drive and we could get here faster. I reckon once I get the route down, we can make up at least 2 hours each way. We could for sure make more trips because we would not be as tired." said John. "Ain't that right Howard."

"Sounds right John." said Howard.

"And what would that cost me?" said Moses.

"I haven't worked that out yet with Howard. He wanted to be sure it was OK with you first."

"That sounds about right to me. You dun good Howard."

"Thank you, kindly Moses. John has a point about more trips. John is a powerful good driver and we could for sure make extra trips with another driver. My contacts in New York have been asking for more merchandise so this could work out well."

"A huh", said Moses, "but I still need to know what this will cost me."

"I was thinking that maybe we could just kept the same fee for each trip. If we make two trips then we get paid for each trip. Howard can share his fee with me. It ain't going cost you nunthin." John said.

"So, the Yankee distributor will pay for each trip and I just need to supply extra merchandise; is that about right?"

"Right as rain Moses." said John.

"So I need to conjure up more cigarettes and guns; that right?" said Moses.

"Right, and more money be comin to you becausin we need more. Right John?" said Howard.

"You bet. Everyone makes out like a bandit." said John.

"This beginin to sound alright to me. This OK with you Howard?" said Moses.

"Yes sir. More money always sounds good to me."

"Well then alright. I will let Howard know when I have the extra merchandise and then we can all make some money."

And that's how it happened. About a week later John and Howard began running double shifts and everyone started making more money.

John made several runs with Howard and after some discussion they decided to split the money 60-40, with John getting the short end because he was new. It was a start, and within a month John hoped that it would be 50-50. It better be because John needed to build up a bankroll just in case. He also needed to start making money for college. Even with a scholarship, if he could get one, he still needed walking around and playing around money.

The runs were easy; drive to some small town in northern South Carolina, then using the special compartments, pack the car with cigarettes and guns. Then they would drive the car back to the distributor's home base where the contents were offloaded. The distributor would off load the merchandise and then pay Howard for the delivery. The only thing that John did not like about the trips was the old 22 pistol that Howard liked to twirl around his finger. If they ever got stopped by the fuzz they would be in even more trouble because of the gun. John had to keep reminding Howard to put the gun away and sometimes Howard did as he was told but often he didn't and that was troubling to John. John could not afford a record of any kind to mar his future plans.

After John came home from the runs, he would take half the money and hide it for emergencies; the other half he put in his mother's dresser drawer. The little extra money that she had was in a middle drawer of the one dresser in the small apartment. She would not remember where this extra money came from, but she probably would guess which was all right with John; he didn't want any credit. He wanted to pay her back for being so good to him. The one bad part of these runs was the fact that he had to act and talk like a redneck like Howard just to get along. He started to mimic Howard's words and tones but it was so foreign to him that he hated it. He hoped that the smuggling would not last long and he could concentrate on school again. John also had another reason to hope that the runs would end soon – his mother.

Rachael was not feeling well and John did not know what to do. The money that John kept putting in her dresser was helping a lot but it was not enough to cover a serious illness. After too long a time when not seeing a doctor, Rachael had finally decided to visit a recommended doctor who would reduce his fee for some patients, but that would not be enough. Both Rachael and John knew that she was very sick and the only question was how sick and what would happen to John. John knew that he was now old enough to live on his own but he could not bear the loss of his mother.

Rachael had an appointment with the doctor for Tuesday. Fortunately, John did not have to make a run that day but John was worried all day at school about what they would find. When he got home he found Rachael at the kitchen table drinking warm tea. She was never home at this time of day so John knew that it was serious.

"Mom, what did the doctor say?"

"It was not good John."

"The doctor said that I have cancer and that it has gone too far for treatment to help; even if I had the money."

John heard the word "cancer" and his entire body got cold. What could he do now and how could he help?

"Is there anything the doctor can do? Can he give you any medicine? He must be able to do something", John practically screamed.

"No John, it is just my time."

John looked at his mother and was horrified at how she looked; she was so small, thin and pale. He could not bear to see her look this way and he could not bear to be alone, but he was afraid that he would be.

John hated to ask this next question but he had to.

"Did the doctor say how long you had?"

"Yes John, he said I would be lucky to last the month."

Now John was not just afraid, he was terrified.

"Mom, I ...", but he could not say anymore. The words would not come out of his dry mouth. For the first time in his short life, John did not know what to say.

"I know John; you are worried about me and what will become of you. So am I. You are smart and I know that you must have a job – that is where the money in the drawer is coming from, right?"

"You will be all right John; you have always been able to make it on your own. I have confidence in you. I just have one request."

"Anything mom, anything you want."

"Whatever is left of my body please have it cremated and throw the ashes in the first ocean that you visit?"

And John said that he would; and he did.

Rachael did not last the month, she lasted 18 days. John did not have the money for a fancy funeral or wake but he did buy his mother a nice dress to wear. It seemed silly to buy a dress that would be burned but John wanted his mother to look pretty, even if only for an hour. The cremation and dress cost him most of the money that he had left but John did not care; it was for his mother and she was worth it. Only a few of Rachael's co-workers came to see her for the last time; most people were afraid to come because they knew that John would be there. It was a simple ceremony that lasted an hour and included some prayers from a local minister. Neither John nor Rachael were what could be called religious but John had heard Rachael pray on several occasions and he wanted someone to pray over his mother at least one time. Whether the prayers helped or not, John could not tell, but he thought that his mother would approve.

It did not take John long to keep the other part of his promise; as soon as he could, he drove to New York and spread his mother's ashes in the Atlantic Ocean. It was the only time in his life that John ever cried.

John would never again cry or truly love any animate object.

CHAPTER 15

After Rachael died John went back to his normal routine of school and his drives with Howard. Now he needed the money more than ever. He continued to make two trips a week and the money that he needed to live on was beginning to build. He would be able to use the extra money when he went to college; which was still on his itinerary. He wanted to go to a good college in order to get a prestigious degree. He also needed a law degree if he wanted to get into politics; almost all politicians were lawyers and the one or two that weren't, wish they were. He also thought about joining the army for a couple of years. Being in the service and having a couple of medals was a good way to make points with his future constituents; but John felt that he could not spare the two or more years that the army would take; besides, he could not take the chance that he could be hurt or killed.

That was a long way off but John would make the time fly by taking college courses in the summer. The trips down south were monotones and talking to Howard for eight hours each way was making John's skin crawl. But something happened one day several months later that changed all that and things were no longer monotonous.

Howard was driving one night on the way south to pick up merchandise and as usual he did not follow John's instructions regarding driving only two miles an hour over the limit. Howard had plans for when he got home to see a local redhead woman who gave good warm blow jobs and so he was hell bent on getting back as soon as he could. Rumor was that she would warm her mouth by eating hot chilies and then when you were done, she would cool you off with Noxzema. People claim that she gave the best blow jobs in the state. As a result of Howard's thoughts and his heavy foot they were stopped on the highway by the state police. The lights and the sirens on the police car pierced the night and woke John from a hazy sleep.

"What's going on?" said John.

"We got caught by the fuzz." said Howard. "I's glad we ain't carrying any merchandize."

Well Howard was right about that. At least if all they got was a ticket they could throw it away later. But Howard was not in any mood to waste time or for a ticket and he definitely did not like cops or blacks.

"Oy wee. Look what we got here John; a coon cop. Did we get lucky or what?"

"Now what can I do for you officer?"

"License and registration please." The cop said.

"Why sure enough; anything for the fuzz."

"Tell me something; you like stopping whiteys? Does it make you feel superior; because you know your not."

"If you are looking for trouble, then you should just keep doing what you are doing."

"Why officer I am just funning; ain't that right John?"

"Sure, you are; you're just a good old boy." But John was starting to get worried. He did not need a police record.

"See that, I'm just a good old boy. See I can be called boy too."

"Mr. Armstrong, your license has expired; I'm going to have to ask you to step out of the car."

John could not believe it; this idiot had an expired license! Man could John pick them. Now John really had to think fast to get out of this mess.

"John, the coon wants me to step out of the car, what do you think I should do?"

"Well I'm thinking strong bout that and I think the cop should just let you go." As if that would happen John thought.

"You're right as rain as usual John." "Officer, I think you should just let me go."

"Please step out of the vehicle." said Officer White.

"Or else what?"

Just then Officer Michael White made the last mistake he would ever make; he reached for his gun. But John was quicker as he took Howard's 22 pistol and shot Officer White twice in the head. Howard was in just as much shock as Officer White but Officer White was dead.

"Damm John, you shot him."

"No shit. What did you expect me to do, dance with him? He's not my type."

"We better get the hell out of here and right quick."

"That sounds like a good idea Howard; let's go."

It took about an hour of driving at a legal speed until they both felt secure enough to speak.

"John what do we do now? You just killed a cop."

"*We* killed a cop. You were there with me or were you having a deep trance or something."

"John lets get the facts straight, you took my gun and you shot the cop."

"If you keep talking like that you will start to worry me. Are you going to turn me in or something?"

John noticed that it took Howard too long to answer the question and he knew that, yes Howard would turn him in to save his own neck. And so he knew what he had to do.

"You are going to turn me in aren't you? You are one sumbitch."

"Now John let's not get all excited, you know I won't do that. Why, we are friends."

But as Howard searched for his pistol, he noticed that it was pointing at him.

"Are you looking for this? Friend."

"OK John I see where you are coming at, but be cool."

"I am cool", said John, as he shot Howard in the chest. The bullet and the gun were old but John's aim was true and Howard died with a bullet in the heart. There would be no warm blow job for Howard tonight.

"Sorry Howard but I just could not take a chance."

And now it was time for John to get as far away as he could. He checked the gun and saw that the pistol still had three bullets in it. That is all he would need.

John had to leave the car because it could be checked back to Howard so he decided to start walking and find another car. Fortunately, it was dark and John was able to hide off the road whenever he heard someone coming. After about five miles of fast walking John came to a small but not tiny town. As he was checking for a car to steal something better came along. She was tall, at least 5' 8", brunette (well you can't have everything), and built (maybe you can). Her name was Suzy and she was 39 years old. She had been married, had one kid, got divorced from her no-account husband and was just getting gas on her way home from work. John played it cool like he usually did.

"Evening Miss." "Can I trouble you for a lift? I am not going far."

"Where are you going?" she asked.

"I ran out of gas just down the road and I am just getting a container of gas now." "I just need a lift to the car."

Suzy looked at the young man and even though she never gave men lifts, he did not look dangerous "OK hop in" she said.

Bad move lady John thought. I wonder if she would have given me a lift if I wasn't good looking. John did not think so. After about two miles Suzy asked, "How much further?"

John took out his gun and said, "This is far enough".

Suzy saw the gun and realized the mistake she made. "Please take the car but let me live." "I have a small boy."

"Good for you. Boys are good to have. OK lady stop the car. Now!"

Suzy did as he said but she was not prepared for what happened next.

"What is your name?" John asked.

"Suzy." she nervously said.

"OK Suzy, pull up off the road under those trees to the left."

"Please, just take the car, I will not tell."

"I almost believe you Suzy but you see I can't take a chance. This has been a big night for me and it seems it isn't over. Now, take off all your clothes and I do mean all and I do mean now."

Now Suzy was more than scared. "Please no, don't hurt me."

"Hurt you? Why this is your big night and I do mean big."

And then John opened his pants and Suzy saw what he meant.

"Oh God no please no, don't hurt me."

"Suzy, Suzy, relax. It's not like you are a virgin or something. A pretty girl like you must have had lots of sex. That's all this is; just good sex. Now hurry with your clothes." John growled.

And Suzy did what she was told to do. And John enjoyed every minute of it. He had her every way that a man could have a woman. She was screaming (in pain, terror, or ecstasy John could not tell) but John shot her in the head anyway. As she was dying John came inside her. John had to admit that this was the best sex that he had ever had. He did not think that he would ever come down but he could not have her again, he was not into dead people. John left her and her clothes by the side of the road and drove to the next town. Now he had to get rid of this car and get another car or get a bus and while he was at it, it was probably best if he got a new id.

At the next town, name unremembered, he ditched the car at a bus parking lot and then washed up at the bus wash room. There were several people in the waiting room and that worked to John's advantage because he probably would not be noticed. John bought a round trip ticket back to school. A round trip ticket was better John thought, because he would not look as suspicious. When the bus came, about 10 minutes late, John slept for the four hours back to class and went straight to sleep. He slept for hours in his room without any care or worry. The only dreams he had was of Suzy and how good she was. He did not think it would ever be that good again. But it was.

Class for John started on Tuesday and he was in no particular hurry for the new semester to begin. He knew that eventually questions would be raised about Howard and since people knew that John and Howard were friends, or at least knew each other, he would be dragged into the conversations. John needed to remember; did anyone see him leave campus with Howard? Think John, think. No, he didn't remember seeing anyone when he left. Is it possible that Howard told anyone that he was leaving with John? That is a big problem and John needed a good answer. Howard would not be that stupid because he knew that they were going for another run and the fewer people that knew the better. John felt that his best option was to get a new identity and get out of town. With his mother dead he really had nothing holding him to this shit hole any way. He had heard that for the right money you could become anyone and he finally had the right money. It was a long time coming but John "Had to get out of Dodge."

CHAPTER 16

John arrived at the alley that he was told to go and he met Manny. Manny was a short, dark, pimply Puerto Rican with lots of connections and no looks. He was just what John needed.

"Listen I need to get new ID's and I heard that you can help. Can you?"

"If you have the right money I can help. Why do you need a new ID?"

"You don't need to know that", said John.

"That's OK; I can tell when someone is having trouble with the police. I can dig it. What exactly do you need?"

"I need everything; birth certificate, license, high school grades, the works."

"Are you going to change your appearance?"

"Do I look like I want to change this face?" said John.

But John though about that and he could see the point. Too many people knew who he was and he could not take the chance that someone would recognize him later, especially when he ran for office.

"Yes, I guess I do need a slight change; not too drastic but enough to not look like me."

"That can be taken care of but how far do you want to go? You said that you need to look different but how different?"

John thought about that and he wondered how far he should go. Changing his hair color would not work because he would always need to color his hair. He thought back to some of the movie star photos that he had seen to try to imagine if he could look like any of them. He also was troubled about the skill of the doctor. How good could he be if he would perform these types of operations? John thought the best approach was to get a second opinion.

"You seem to have had a lot of experience in these matters, what would you do if you were me?"

"Do you expect to leave town and move away? How many people know you and could recognize you?" questioned Manny.

"Depending on the papers you get for me I intend to register at a college that is far away. I don't have any family and the only people that know me are in this town." And John thought that at least he was lucky in that regard.

"That makes it easy. You can even get by with no change if you don't think anyone will ever see you again."

John thought about that and he knew that he could not risk it. What would happen when he ran for national office? No, he needed a change, a change that could pass inspection but one that would not ruin his "good looks".

"OK I have made up my mind. Let's go for a change, a change that no one could detect. How good is the doctor you use?"

"Good enough. He has done this before; he is a professional and has an operating room that he can use, but it won't be cheap."

"Gee really, I figured that. I assume that he wants it all up front and doesn't take insurance, as if I had any."

"That can be taken care of. You can get insurance papers with your documents and you can use those papers for the operation. The doctor will take care of that for you." said Manny

This was beginning to sound like it might work after all so Kevin made the appointment to meet the doctor for the next day. He did not like the idea of leaving town and all his "friends" but he really had no choice. Someone would eventually put two and two together and not come up with three.

CHAPTER 17

Dr. "Jones" was an easy-going man in his late fifties. The little hair he still had had tuned steel gray along with his small mustache and goatee. He was heavy but not obese, medium height and had the smooth hands of a surgeon with skin so pale that they were almost translucent. His office was in a two-story building just at the far edge of town. He was a good plastic surgeon that by rights should be performing his magic in a large famous hospital where he would be paid obscene fees for making old rich people look like young rich people and for making rich fat people look rich and thin. If it wasn't for that botched operation that he made one late evening after drinking too many Mai Tai's he probable still would. He consoled himself with the knowledge that he wasn't suppose to be on duty the night that a tractor trailer crashed into a van of sleepy school kids coming home from camp. "I should have refused to operate" he thought, but because of his arrogance and belief in his skills a young eight-year girl named Shirley was dead. The formal review inquiry regarding the operation cleared him of wrong doing, which was better than he deserved, and the money that he lost in the following law suit was less than he deserved. Now he was a hired gun for a mid-level crook. Instead of making people young he made new people. People came to him, not to look new but for a new look. This would be his career from now on and he hated it.

There was an emergency operation scheduled for the next day and Dr. Jones knew what that meant; someone was in a hurry to get out of town. The phony insurance forms he used would pay for the operation and then some but he would never again make the fees that he was used to receiving. He would never again drive a big car or drink expensive vodka or be able to afford the best call girls. At his age and limited money, he would probably have to get used to a used Honda, weak booze, and lonely evenings.

Tomorrow's patient was in the waiting room for a pre-operation evaluation. One look at the young boy and he could not believe what he was seeing. "This was Rachael's son." he thought; "Why does he need an operation? What did he do wrong?" But then the doctor remembered John's history and he did not need to think about the reason anymore. "It was bound to happen sooner or later with that kid." he thought. "Well, a fee is a fee." But he did not realize that John had other thoughts; John did not want or need any witnesses.

"Good morning doctor," said John.

The doctor played it cool and did not let on that he knew John; to be more accurate he knew Rachel. He was the one who took care of Rachel when she got sick. He was the only doctor that took these mercy cases for little or no money. Dr Jones was not an oncologist but he knew the tests and did the best he could for the indigent patients. This was his way of paying back for his mistake. His work with the poor in his mind mitigated what he now did to make a living.

"Good morning. How can I help you today?" said Dr. Jones.

"I am looking for a change that would not damage my looks but make me unrecognizable. Can you do that?"

"I can do that. Let me show you some diagrams of changes that I can make and I'll let you decide which one is best for you. Are you in a hurry for this change?" asked Dr. Jones.

"Why are you asking? Is it important to know that?" asked John.

Now the doctor was worried, John asked his question with just enough hidden anger to make Dr. Jones sorry that his mother had ever conceived. Dr. Jones had to use tact to respond or he could make John even angrier.

"Yes, it is. I have other operations to schedule and I was asked to schedule yours for tomorrow. I was just curious as to why you need an operation that fast. If you don't want to tell me that is all right; I understand you and I will still perform the operation tomorrow. Lots of people want to have the operation right away."

John wanted to keep the doctor in the dark as best as possible and he did not want any questions asked. John thought about the response he should give and he felt that it was best to just be non-confrontational; for now.

"Sorry doctor, all I can say is that I would like to have the operation tomorrow, if you are available. Is that OK with you?"

"Yes, it is. Why don't you look at the pictures and we can go from there." said the doctor as he quietly sighed with relief.

John took the pictures from the doctor and began his evaluation of the pictures, the doctor and the office. Thoughts were running through his mind about the quality of them all. He was also planning how to eliminate the doctor and Manny; he could not afford any witnesses and the process needed to be done soon after the operation.

As he looked at the pictures one stood out. One of the diagrams looked like it could work out better than the others. It was a less major change than the others and the healing would not take as long. The operation would involve a change to his nose and chin, both of which John liked as they were, but John felt that this was the best choice.

"Doctor, I think this change would not be too radical, what do you think?"

The doctor looked over the photo that John handed him and he was impressed at the choice John made. He really is as smart as I have heard, he thought; this change would be easy, heal quickly and make a dramatic change in John's appearance. The change might actually make John more handsome then he already was.

"Good selection. This would not be that dramatic an operation but you would definitely look different. What say we schedule this for nine AM tomorrow?"

"I'll be here on time." said John.

And he was on time. The operation was performed in a small operating room in back that was just large enough to hold one table. The room was clean and the instruments looked like they were sterilized so John relaxed as best that he could. Fortunately for John, the doctor did all the work by himself; he did not use an anesthesiologist or assistant. This meant that later, after he recovered, John only had to eliminate two people with two bullets; an easy day's work.

CHAPTER 18

John's face was healing well and he felt that the time was right to make his escape, but first he needed to make one more trip; he needed to get Manny and Dr. Jones together and eliminate them. John still had the gun that he used to kill Howard and there were still two bullets left; and that was all John needed.

Manny had done a good job with the fake documents and John was sure that he could make this work. After he eliminated his two witnesses, he would use a beat-up Ford that he recently bought and drive to Boston to start his new life. John's mind was working overtime with different ideas on the elimination process. The easiest way was to get them both together in a lonely spot and put one bullet in each head; but how to get them together? John believed that Manny and the doctor seldom met or discussed business unless it was necessary; therefore, John had to make the meeting necessary. John also had the nagging feeling the doctor recognized him in the office and that was another reason why the doctor had to go. John finally decided on a plan of attack. John would tell Manny that he was unhappy with the results of the operation and tell Manny to schedule a meeting with Manny and the doctor. John was not sure if Manny would agree because John had already paid for the surgery but it was worth a try; sometimes you get lucky.

As John suspected Manny was none too happy with John's request for a meeting but when John told Manny that he would write an anonymous letter to the police, Manny had to agree to a meeting.

"Hey man that's not how it works, you dig. You got the service and there are no refunds." said Manny.

"I'm not looking for a refund I just am not happy with the work. What kind of quack doctor are you using?" John said.

"Quack doctor, man, are you kidding?" said Manny.

"This is one of the best plastic surgeons in the business. Before the doc had a little trouble, he was one of the highest paid in the business. If you had this operation in a regular hospital, it would have cost you twice as much; and that does not count the paper work. Man, we do good work and come recommended you know what I'm saying?'

"I just have some concerns and I want to speak to the doctor, that's all. It will be a short meeting and we can straighten everything out."

Manny had a lot of doubt but he really had no choice; he could not let this kid report his operation to the police so he said he would try to setup the meeting. That was not as easy as he expected because Doctor Jones had major concerns about seeing John again.

"No way do I want to meet this kid." he thought. "I have a bad feeling that for whatever reason he has for the facial change, he must want to get rid of witnesses."

The doctor did his best trying to cancel out of the meeting but Manny kept insisting.

"Hey doc, this kid wants to report us, you understand? That would not help our arrangement. Let's just go to the one meeting and quiet this kid down."

"To be honest." said the doctor; "I don't trust him. I recognize him and I have heard all bad things about him. If he wants to change his appearance that can only mean one thing – he's in trouble. And if he's in trouble then he may want to eliminate anyone who can recognize him. I really don't want to meet him without protection." said the doctor.

"What you going to have sex with him? Is that why you need protection?" said Manny.

"Come on you know what I mean."

"Yes, I do and maybe I can help. I do have a new .45 caliber that will give you lots of protection. No matter how bad he is, this will stop him."

Manny was not as sure as he sounded. If this guy was as bad as the doc said then they could be in trouble even with a gun.

The meeting was set for the next afternoon late in the day. John wanted it to be dark but not as dark that they would not want to come.

Manny and the doctor looked so peaceful; almost as if they were asleep, but their eyes were open. Manny's mouth was open in a big oval but the doctor's mouth was closed and had a dribble of blood on his left lip. Both Manny and the doctor had a small hole in their respective chests and neither would ever see the light of day again.

PART 11
Peter Marks

CHAPTER 1

And John died and Peter Marks was born. He looked somewhat similar but just different enough that with any luck no one would recognize him. His new papers worked fine and he would now be a freshman in Harvard. That was no easy task because Harvard, even in those days, was one of the most difficult schools to get into. Harvard was an interesting place; it is one the oldest university in America and has an impressive list of alumni. Peter was able to be accepted by Harvard because his grades were inflated as well as his entrance grades. Manny did a very good job with these documents; too bad he would never be able to get documents again.

Now he could start his real life and begin his climb to the top. This would be especially difficult for Peter because he had to hide his prior name and life. He also had to hope that no one would recognize him with his new appearance. The transcripts that he used were so good that even Peter could not tell they were phony. He did have to change his birthday otherwise he might be considered too young for admission into Harvard. That would make him two years older than he really was, but it should not be a problem to Peter's plans. And Peter had plans – first Harvard, then Harvard Law, then politics. He hoped that he could have a little fun along the way but that was not important to his plans. He would take whatever came his way. And it would.

With his mother gone the only thing that Peter had left was his ambition – and he had lots of ambition. Eventually he would need a wife; that would make politics easier, but that could wait. He did not need the problem of a wife when he had to concentrate on classes. Peter knew that there were plenty of women on campus and he could have his choice but there would be no long-term commitment for him. If it wasn't for his ambition, he did not think that he would ever get married; who needed the trouble. Like they say; "If you're getting the milk, why buy the cow?"

He would be good within reason; after all, even good boys can't be good all the time. As Saint Augustine said "Give me chastity and continence, but not yet."

Harvard was an interesting place; it was bigger than he expected and cost lots more money. Peter needed more than one part time job to pay his way because he could not get a scholarship. Harvard is a private university located in Cambridge Massachusetts and it is the oldest institute of higher learning in the US. Because Peter was a first-year student he stayed in a dormitory near Harvard Yard.

First year seemed like it would last forever but sometimes you need to spent the time if you want to make the dimes.

CHAPTER 2

Portia had started high school and she had lots of friends. The girls liked her because they wanted to be near the prettiest girl in school and the boys from the nearby school liked her because she was the prettiest girl in school. Some of the girls resented the looks that Portia received from the boys, but Portia had such a good way about her that she eventually put them at ease. The other girls wanted to be her friend so that they could get her male rejects.

She would continue to get straight A's in class but she would not flaunt it. She did not want people to think she was smart because that would make her lose her mystic. People thought that she was just a pretty face and body and that made it easy for her to get her way. Some of the teachers in class looked at her in ways that made her smirk and made her nauseous. Even if Portia were not as smart, as the teachers were, she would be able to smile and get any grade that she wanted from those dirty old men. It was amazing what you can get away with when you were beautiful; men are so easy, she thought.

Portia's high school years were coming to an end and she was looking forward to college. She would be going to Harvard, the same as her father. Her mother, a socialite, never went to college; she went to a finishing school instead. Portia really did not need or want to go to college but she went because it made her father happy and whatever else she was, she was still daddy's girl.

Portia was thinking ahead to college. What would it be like at a large university and how different would it be from the small schools that she was used to? It would definitely be more crowed and more noisy and more hectic.

CHAPTER 3

As with grade school and high school, Harvard was not a big challenge for Peter. Most of the classes were dull as were the professors. Many professors, especially at a university such as Harvard, have a world of academic experience and have tenure, but little if any real-world experience. They taught the theories and concepts and that was all. And it would have to do. Peter only needed the paper that said he graduated with honors; whatever he learned would be gravy. Peter would do whatever it took to graduate with honors and he did not care if he learned a single thing. These four years would go by slowly because he needed to work in between semesters. Money was slow to come but fast to go and he needed to find and make as much as he could. Peter wished that he could have saved some money from the operation and the fake papers, but that was the best that he could do on short notice.

CHAPTER 4

Portia had entered Harvard with straight A's but she was very nonchalance about her intelligence. She did not want to let anyone know that she was smarter than them. As in high school, she wanted people to believe that she was just a "dumb blonde". Portia did not believe that she needed a college education but if she was to meet an appropriate mate this college was the place to be. Only the very rich or the very smart or with connections attended Harvard and her father would accept that in a match for his only daughter. She also needed the business training in order to take over the company. Her father took her to work whenever he could and whenever Portia was available but with both their schedules, timing was difficult. The family would vacation in the summer in their modest house in Newport Rhode Island. The house and property were not as large as the complex outside Philadelphia but it was adequate for socializing. This was another way that she was introduced to the right people.

CHAPTER 5

Philip DeMarco was a cop for 5 years, and he still loved being a cop. He was a former marine and reached the rank of Gunnery Sergeant before he left the Corp. Like most retired marines, he would always consider himself a marine, "Once a marine always a marine" as the saying goes. When he moved to Erie, he quickly joined the police department and was now a well-respected homicide detective. Most homicide detectives will tell you that it takes a special person to solve murders. You needed patience and a good eye to see things that others could not see. You also needed a strong stomach. Some murders were so gruesome that even experience cops could not handle it. Philip remembered a case where a father raped and battered his three-year-old daughter. The child was beaten so badly that you could not tell that she was a girl. No one would have been upset if Philip had beaten the father to death but of course he could not do that. He was too good a cop. The father was eventually found guilty by reason of insanity and was sent to a hospital. What they should have done was put him in jail and let the inmates take care of him, thought Philip. Even in those days, the law took unexpected turns.

Philip, or "Guns" as he was usually called because of his service and rank as a marine, was looking over the case of three people who were murdered in North Carolina. This was obviously not his jurisdiction but sometimes he looked at these cases to see if they had any similarity with cases that he was working on. One person killed was a cop, which immediately got his attention. The cop was shot at close range after a traffic stop. According to the reports, the cop, his name was Michael White, called in a traffic stop but then never followed up on the call. What made the case so interesting is that Officer White called in the license plate number for the car and that same car, with a dead driver, was found 60 miles away. The driver was shot with the same caliber bullet as Officer

White. To top that off, 15 miles further away a young woman, Suzy was her name, was found raped and shot with the same caliber bullet. This sure looked like the same person killed all three people. Philip was reading about the case and something was troubling him. What kind of person could kill with such ease? But he did not know the answer. Some maniac was out on the street killing and no one could find him. Philip had enough on his plate that he could not get involved even if he could but he keeps this information in the top drawer of his brain where it might come in handy someday.

On the way home to his quiet, small, and lonely apartment that resided on a dusty corner of a small street, Philip keep thinking about the triple murder. He had brought some files home and after a microwave dinner of non-descript fast food and a reasonably cold beer he would look at the files again. He had nothing else to do. Life as a marine and then as a detective did not lead itself to having stable relationships. He was married for a few years but that did not last long. Before he got married his career as a marine sent him to foreign locations, sometimes to fight, but once he got married, he was lucky enough to stay on one base. That made his wife Monica very happy. Monica was a pretty, almost beautiful, blond that Philip met by accident. He liked to say that it was the best accident he ever had. He was in his marine kakis and she was a civilian secretary for one of the base captains. They met over a spilt coffee at the PX and she was taken by him because he was so nice about the mess she made. He told her that the uniform could be washed and that she should not worry about the stains. "Marines know how to wash clothes," he told her. They sat down together, him in his wet clothes and Monica in a soft pastel dress and they talked for what seemed liked hours. They talked for the entire lunch hour and more until Philip used his strength to ask her to dinner. He was more than shocked when she said yes. At dinner they talked as if they knew each other for years. It was almost as if they were the same person even though they were so different. Philip did not remember what he ate, or even if he ate, but he remembered everything about Monica. What she wore, how she smelled, and her beautiful smile. She had the same smile that all beautiful women had. It just lit up a room and it would light up his life.

Philip could never understand what she saw in him. He was so different from "his flower" as he called her. She was quiet, reserved, and feminine and he was a marine gunny. But they fell in love and got married. It was a simple marriage with just a few close friends and it was exactly what they wanted, no pomp or fancy party. Both had small families that were invited to the ceremony and intimate dinner. Philip wished that he could do more, but Monica did not want or need any more; she was happy with the ceremony and small diamond ring he gave her just like it was. Monica wore a simple wedding dress and Philip wore his dress uniform with his many medals. Everyone commented about how beautiful Monica looked and how happy Philip looked. Philip would never be that happy again.

Like many people, they went to Niagara Falls for their honeymoon. They enjoyed the sights, the food, and being together. During the day they took the boat that rides close to the falls and Philip took a picture of Monica in her rain slicker; he called it his "Maid of the Mist" picture. At night they made soft, sweet love and went to sleep in each other's arms. It was the best time of his life and he never wanted it to end and he never wanted to leave. He hoped that they could grow old together. They probably would have beaten the odds and made it except for the truck that cut Monica's life short. Philip was home at the base when it happened. Monica had gone out shopping for food and never returned. He never expected that the marines coming to his house would announce his wife's death and not his. Meeting her was the best accident in his life and this was the worse. He never got over her death and he knew that he never would. He also knew that no other woman could take her place. It seemed as if the accident had happened yesterday, but it was six years ago and Philip had not dated since and he knew that he never would. He left the marines soon after the accident and moved away to try to forget, but it didn't work; he could never forget; and he did not want to forget.

Becoming a cop seemed to be a good idea because as best as possible, it helped keep his mind off Monica. He was a good cop with just a hint of the toughness that he carried over from his marine days. He worked hard at the job in order to forget and as a result it was not long before he was made detective. Like many cops Philip smoked but, in his case, he almost hoped that the cigarettes would kill him. Deep down Philip could not live without Monica. He knew that dying was not the answer and giving up was not a choice for a marine but he was just depressed all the time. He hoped that there was a heaven and when he died, he would be reunited with Monica. That was his wish, his dream, and his fantasy. It was the only thing that kept him going. Just in case, and to be sure, every night he prayed and asked God to let him be reunited with Monica and every morning he woke up. Sometimes God does not answer prayer.

CHAPTER 6

Peter was getting lucky on campus. Women had a nickname for him – "Peter Pecker" and he liked the name. His skill in class and out of class was serving him well. He could not skip classes like he did before but he could take lots of classes and perhaps finish early. With luck, and by going to school in the summers, he expected to finish his four-year degree in three. Then he would apply for law school. That would not be easy because he needed to take a special law entrance exam and he needed a high-grade point average. The grade point average was easy because he was a straight A student. Money problems were another issue. Without his job transporting cigarettes and guns Peter needed to find local work to pay for rent, food, and school. Between classes and work he also needed to study for the law exam. He would use all his spare time to study for the entrance exam and work a part time job. The part time job, at a local insurance office, was working out fine for Peter. The work was easy; the hours fit his schedule, and the female boss (not too shabby looking) was very interested in his 'big mind." All things considered; college so far was not bad; not bad at all.

The money that Peter made at the insurance agency was small compared to the money that he made with Howard but at least there was no long drive and Peter did not have to listen to and smell Howard. But he needed another source of income and he needed it soon.

CHAPTER 7

Peter was slowly running out of patience with his roommate. Jacob was a snob a slob and a Jew. Three for three, could it get any worse? How does the school make its decisions on room sharing, throw darts at a board?" thought Peter. But Peter knew that was not true. Harvard took great pains to pick people that would be best suited for each other based on a very long questionnaire that they fill out before admissions. Peter filled out the questionnaire the way that he assumed the school expected and so he should not have been surprised by what kind of roommates he got. But now Peter had to get a new roommate and soon.

Peter remembered that in the spring, as a member of the incoming class, he received a mailing that included an application for first-year housing and an adviser information form. The housing application asks freshmen to fill in some objective criteria such as estimated waking and sleeping hours, preferences for quiet or social settings, tastes in music, and expectations of neatness. The adviser's form inquiries about possible fields of concentration, academic strengths and weaknesses, and interests outside the classroom. Peter was also asked to write a short essay describing himself and the characteristics he would like for his roommates to possess. How about a 19-year-old female blonde nymph? Do you have any of those? What a waste!

Class was easy but not so easy that Peter could just coast. Some of the classes, OK many of the classes, were of no use to him or any one; but he had to take them. Required and all that. He did like the cut of the women. College was better than high school in that regard. The women in college were probably more experienced in the ways of sex; but if they weren't Peter would be glad to help them. There was one animal in his American History class, another in English Lit, and one that was taking an Advanced Algebra class. Advanced Algebra? Why in the world would any women take that class? "Women don't need to learn math. They just needed to learn to count to nine inches." he thought. And he could help them in that regard.

CHAPTER 8

Peter was now a junior and getting bored already. He knew that he needed a degree from college and then a law degree but it just seemed to be taking too long. And then there was Jacob. Peter needed a way to, at the very least; get him out of this room. He knew that if he killed again, he would run the risk of getting caught but he had to do something.

Peter knew from his all-religion calendar that one of the big Jewish holidays was coming up and that Jacob would be going home to mommy. The school of course would be closed as it usually is for Jewish holidays; so many teachers are Jewish, and Peter thought that he might have a way to solve this problem at that time. It had to look like an accident and it had to be good; no one could trace it to him and no one could think it was murder. What to do, Peter was wondering? I really need to think now. If he sabotaged the car, it might be found out. Could he hire someone to kill Jacob in a robbery attempt? No. Peter knew that if you want to kill you needed to do it yourself; no witnesses. Jacob was a heavy smoker and Peter remembered that nicotine in some form could kill you. Not cigarettes but in pure form. No, that would be trouble because Peter did not know where to get that form of nicotine and that would require a witness. Peter felt the best way out was by accident. Cars have accidents all the time he thought and this would just be another unfortunate accident.

Of course, Peter knew about cars; he read many automobile manuals in his spare time, so he knew how to drain different fluids from a car. He could not drain all the brake fluid of course because Jacob could tell by the feel of the brakes that something was wrong; but if he drained some of the fluid or made a cut in the line that could work. And so Peter began to organize a plan.

CHAPTER 9

Kevin had gotten the best grades in school and he had been accepted to Penn State at Erie, the Behrend College. He would be the first from his tribe to enter this prestigious university. He was already a sophomore and with lots of hard work, getting good grades. After he finished his political science degree he would transfer to Philadelphia Law and then the hard work would start. Kevin was good, but was he good enough for these schools? Both would require work and concentration and more money than he had. He was able to get a part scholarship through the Bureau of Indian Affairs but it would not be enough. He still needed extra funds for books and room and board. He could work at Kane in the summer months but he really wanted to use the summer to prepare for the law entrance exam and to see his family. His parents were not getting any younger and neither was his grandfather. He was becoming very concerned with his grandfather JC. JC was in his 80's now and was having difficulty walking and the cold winters were not doing his body any good. The family had been preparing for the day when JC was gone and it looked like that day would be soon. JC wondered why everyone was concerned with his health. Death was a normal part of life. It was just another length of road to travel. JC would miss his family of course but he would not miss the pains from old age. He never thought that he would last as long as he did but he was glad that he had. He lived long enough to see his family survive and do well and he lived long enough to see Kevin enter college. It would take a miracle for JC to see Kevin finish law school but he did not need to worry, Kevin would make it.

CHAPTER 10

Portia was beginning to like Harvard. It was hard but she could handle the work; after all, she had good genes and study habits. Like high school, the boys were very attracted to her and she always had a swarm of men around her. She could smell the testosterone and the sweet smell of sweat all day and she still loved what she was doing to the men. She still was able to twist the boys and men around her finger and she was still a virgin. She never found anyone that met her two criteria's for having first sex; when she wanted to and with whom she wanted. And then she saw Peter Marks. And Peter saw her and it was lust at first sight for both of them. Peter had never seen anyone as beautiful as Portia and Portia had never seen anyone that met her two criteria before. Portia was smart and knew about men but she was naïve when it came to sex. She wanted to learn but she also wanted to be careful. She had heard about diseases that you can catch and she was not going to catch any. One look at Peter and she could tell that he was no virgin but she had to be careful and play her cards right. But she didn't realize that Peter had a bigger deck.

Portia was interested in Peter but Peter was playing it smooth and was letting her guess his next move. Peter knew enough about women that he could tell when someone was very interested in him; and Portia was very interested in him. Because they were not in the same class or year at school Peter had to make his move during breaks or after class. There were plenty of places where Peter could affect an unexpected meeting and that would be Peter's approach. He noticed that Portia spent a lot of time at the library, with good reason; it was one of the largest and best libraries in the world. Peter decided that he would frequent the library more than usual and study in one of the study areas. With any luck she would make the first move. Peter did not even know her name but he could tell her type. The way she dressed indicated that she came from money; the way she walked indicated that she whey to an expensive finishing school, but the way she studied was puzzling. He could not figure out why she needed to study so hard; why did she even need to go to school? With her good looks she could find a good husband and Harvard is the place for that.

CHAPTER 11

The plan for Peter and Portia was working. They both wanted to meet and the accidental bump in the library set the stage. Since they were both interested it made it easy to start taking. Each was a good talker and listener, Because the library was open late on most nights they talked for hours. Portia was careful not to give too much away about her finances and Peter did not have much to give away. Peter did mention that he wanted to be a lawyer. Portia could do better on that account like maybe an accountant who could work at her father's firm but lawyer was not that bad.

Peter had been dating Portia now for two weeks and he finally took the big step that he felt would lead to a big night, sex.

Since Portia was a virgin, she let Peter teach her, and he did. She did not realize what she was missing because she did not have any experience. She wondered if all men were this good. She actually had what she would find out later was an orgasm. Peter was smart enough to not try any of his usual activity in bed because he did not know how Portia would take them but after a few sessions he would get more active. He never had a virgin before and it really made him hot and hard.

When people saw Peter with Portia both the men and women were jealous. Everyone agreed that they made a great couple and they probably had a good future. But they did not.

CHAPTER 12

After several months of dating and medium good sex for him, Peter had finally made the decision. He would ask Portia to marry him. He didn't really love her but at least she was a good piece of ass and she had money. He could tell by how good Portia's mother looked (Oh yes, Peter would like to do her) that Portia would probably age well. Now that he was an honest and lawyer is that an oxymoron) he needed a family to get to the next level. He was going to run for representative this year and a beautiful wife was a great asset. He would easily win this contest and with luck only need to serve two terms before he ran for either Governor or the Federal senate. Senator had a nice ring to it but as governor he would have a better chance of becoming President. That was his ultimate goal: the top dog, big cheese, king of the hill, President. And he had lots of ideas on what he could do as President.

He planned the evening in such a way that Portia would never turn down his proposal. They had dinner at a popular restaurant, then dancing at a local jazz club that Portia loved, drinks back in her apartment, then presenting her with flowers and the ring. The ring was the best he could afford with his salary but it was adequate. It was one carat with two rectangular baguettes in a silver setting. It was just large enough without being ostentatious. And then after an hour of two of bodies sweating on silk sheets, they would fall asleep in each other arms. Not a bad way to end a day and start a better life with a beautiful wife.

Peter had everything going for him: good looks, a beautiful wife, education from a good school and with his marriage would come money; lots of money; enough to buy his first election. That is how it is done today, make a lot of money, get elected, and then make LOTS of money. Money would give him power and being a politician would give him lots of power. What is that phrase that Peter heard before; "Power corrupts and absolute power corrupts absolutely." He knew that was true and he could not wait to become even more corrupt. And, as said in a movie "There is no Good or Evil just power." But he did have one problem. He knew that he could not get by with a simple wedding. Portia came from too important a family and they would expect and require an elaborate wedding.

"Why can't we just elope," he asked himself. "We could even just go to city hall and get the stupid piece of paper."

But he knew that could not happen. He would have the required engagement party then the shower and then the big wedding. What a waste of money he thought. I could put that money to better use. And then he had the bigger problem, who could he invite from his side of the family? He had no family that he knew of and as this new person he really had no family. The best idea was to just say that he had no family. He was not sure if anyone would believe him but for once it was the truth. He was going to tell people that his parents died in a car accident and because the family moved around, he did not know if he had any other family. That was as good excuse as he could come up with and he hoped that it was good enough. It would have to be good enough.

CHAPTER 13

Portia was walking on air; Peter had proposed! Actually, he did more than propose; he used her like he never used her before and for once she did not stop him. She was a little disgusted with herself for the things that she did, but she could not stop herself, she was too much in love; at least she thought that it was love because she had never been in love before. Peter was the first man that she was with and she had no way of knowing what she really was feeling except she knew that she was happy. Portia was happy but she was not sure how her father would respond.

CHAPTER 14

As soon as she arrived home, she could not wait to tell her father.

"Dad, I have good news, Peter asked me to marry him." Portia laughed.

Andrew knew Peter because they had diner together several times and once Andrew and Portia were treated to dinner at a local Italian restaurant. Something about Peter made Andrew unhappy about Portia dating Peter and now he had proposed. Peter did not even have the curtesy to ask Andrew for Portia's hand. And Andrew's body turned cold. He had very serious reservations about Peter and he did not want Peter as a son-in-law. He hired some of the best private investigators in the business but they could not find any information about Peter; it was as if his life started at age nineteen. There was no information about Peter before he was nineteen. Oh, there were documents that said he attended schools, etc., but when the investigators checked, no one had ever heard of him. It was almost as if Peter dropped down from the sky fully formed. There was something very sinister about him and Andrew did not want Peter to marry his only child. But Andrew also knew that he could not just tell Portia "No", that might cause her to have to choose between himself and Peter and Andrew could not bear to hear her choice.

CHAPTER 15

Portia could not believe that her father did not approve of Peter. Peter was such a perfect catch. He was tall, handsome, humorous, had a great future, and he was great in bed. What more could he want for a son-in-law; better yet, what more could she want? Yes, Peter did not have any money and yes, he had no family but he had great potential because of his education and he didn't need any money because he had Portia's money. And that was the big problem. Edward believed that Peter only wanted Portia because of her money and the money she would inherit. Edward knew that he could always give Peter a high-level job in his real estate firm, but Peter knew nothing about real estate. His law degree would be in government law and not real estate law. This meant that most likely Peter would need to start at the bottom of the corporate latter as a junior associate at some large law firm and he would not be able to make the kind of money that would support Portia in the style that she had grown accustomed. Although Portia loved her father, she was beginning to realize that she might have to choose between her father and Peter and she was afraid of what would happen if she made the wrong decision. Would her father disinherit her if she defied him; could she live without Peter?

It took Portia so long to find a perfect match that she just could not think about loosing Peter but she could not stand to lose her father either. This decision was giving her headaches and causing friction at home. Her father did not yell or raise his voice but it was clear by the way that he talked that he did not like Peter and Portia could not tell why. She wanted to ask but she was afraid of what he might say. What if Peter had a dark secret, would she want to know? The answer was no. She could not afford to lose the best thing that she ever wanted.

CHAPTER 16

Andrew knew that the day was coming when Portia would tell him that Peter and she wanted to get married, but the day came too soon. Portia was in love with love and did not realize what a bad choice she was making and Andrew did not know how to tell his only child that she was ruining her life. His wife was of no use; she thought that Peter was a good match, but what was she making that decision on? Andrew knew that the harder he fought this marriage the more Portia would resent him and that might mean that she would move away and Andrew might never see any grandchildren. The one thing that Andrew wanted more than anything was a granddaughter to play with and to love and he could not risk losing that even if it hurts his only daughter.

CHAPTER 17

Just as Peter thought, Portia did have an engagement party but this one was even bigger that he expected. It seemed that everyone in society wanted to be there and they were. The party cards requested no gifts just a donation to her favorite charity, the Cancer Society. Portia's aunt Portia, who she was named after, died of breast cancer so she was partial to that organization. Befitting her status each table had a fancy favor and a large vase full of white roses on it. It was one of the most opulent parties anyone had ever seen.

Andrew wanted to give his daughter a special gift for the engagement but he kept it a secret.

He decided to give her the Walther PPK gun used by James Bond in so many memorable movies. This gun was light enough for Portia to use if the occasion occurs which Andrew hoped would never occurs. Portia had training on how to shoot in fact, she was very good with a shotgun. She often beat her father when they would shoot at the skeet grounds. She liked the gift so much that she wound up carrying it in her purse. Just for emergencies.

CHAPTER 18

As Peter expected, the engagement party was followed with a shower. Portia had a shower, why he did not know. The shower was for women only and there was over 60 women who were invited and who came. Some of the women who came were friends of Portia from school and who also knew Peter from bed so they knew about "Peter Pecker" and were jealous but they all agreed that they made a great couple, if only they knew.

CHAPTER 19

Kevin had just finished college and because of his college grades, his grades on the LSAT, and his status as a minority he was easily admitted to Philadelphia University Law School. Although his parents wanted him to dress more like a "normal" American and to cut his hair short, Kevin refused to conform; he was an Indian and he was proud of it. Looking different, especially at a place like Philadelphia University, was not that big a deal. It was not as if he wore shorts or buckskins to class; he wore conservative clothes but kept his hair long and neat. There was no question to anyone that he was an Indian and no one cared.

This was the summer before he entered law school and he was driving back home with his old Ford truck with so many miles on it that the odometer was on its second life. As he was driving and thinking of seeing family and friends again, he saw a car younger than his truck and with a fresh coat of paint and driving it was John.

Kevin could still not get John out of his mind. Was that really him that he saw on the road and if it was why did he change his appearance? And Kevin recognized John right away. And he knew that John might have recognized him as well. Why in the world was he hiding and did he have a different name? Should Kevin go up to him and ask how he was doing? No, Kevin did not think that was a good idea. For whatever reason John had for his appearance it meant that he did not want to be found. Whatever reason that John had, Kevin would not interfere. But he would try to find out what was going on. Kevin wondered if he should contact the cop that he met after his accident but Kevin was not sure of his name (Pete, Philip) or whether that was a good idea. John was not someone to be trifled with but the cop thought that John was guilty of something, perhaps murder.

CHAPTER 20

Kevin had been driving for years both at home and at school. You learn to drive at an early age at an Indian reservation. There still were horses on the reservation but most people drove old cars and trucks. They drove the vehicles until they stopped working and could not be fixed and then they found another old truck or car to take its place. No one was rich enough to buy a new car or even better a truck. He considered himself a good driver; he never drove after drinking, and he was a defensive driver. None of that prepared him for the speeder that rammed his car one cold fall night in the highway from Penn to Erie. Both cars and both drivers were hurt in the collision with Kevin's car taking the bulk of the crash. It was only an old, beat-up, green pickup that Kevin maintained and that still got Kevin to where he was going but Kevin hated to lose it. The other driver suffered bruises and Kevin had a broken arm. As usual, the person that caused the accident did not suffer as much damage as the people in the other vehicle.

The first cop on the scene was a detective who happened to be on his way home from work. Detective Philip DeMarco stopped and called in the report on his car radio. Within ten minutes an ambulance and fire truck both arrived on the scene almost simultaneously. Kevin went to the hospital to have his arm set and Philip followed to get information on the accident. It was a normal accident involving two vehicles and Detective DeMarco took the information down quickly. Detective DeMarco was very impressed with how calm Kevin appeared to be after such an experience. Normally someone in an accident, especially when they are hurt, is very agitated, but Kevin was calm and very much in control. The detective found Kevin interesting and easy to talk to. He was just what the detective needed to take his mind off Monica for awhile. While Kevin was having his arm set Philip began to talk to Kevin about things other than the accident.

Kevin was very easy to talk to and Philip was eager to listen. Kevin spoke about college and how he intended to be a lawyer one day and Philip remarked in jest, "Just what we need - another lawyer." Kevin told him about a student that disappeared years ago and Philip took notice of the dates. That was just about the time that the three people were killed. Now Philip was very interested in what Kevin had to say. Philip asked Kevin if he knew someone named Howard Armstrong and Kevin replied that Howard was a student at his high school. When Philip asked about John and Kevin replied in the affirmative Philip became wide awake. Going home was no longer important; Philip had to find out everything that Kevin knew about John and Howard.

"Kevin, I need to ask you some important questions regarding Howard and John Water. Do you remember if they knew each other? Were they friends?"

"John did not have any friends. For a short while in grade school John spoke to me but that was it. I do remember seeing John and Howard together at high school. They did seem to know each other and they both seemed to be missing from school at the same time."

"Around the time when Howard was killed did John ever return to class?" asked Philip

"Now that you mention it, I do remember that John did not return around the same time that Howard turned up murdered. At the time I was suspicious but what could I have said or done?"

"Kevin, this is kind of important, do you have any idea where John could have gone? Did he have any family or friends?"

"Absolutely not; his mother passed just two months before John disappeared and as far as I can remember he had no other family or friends. He was not a friendly person. I often wondered what happened to him. He was very smart in school but not a nice person."

"What do you mean, 'Not a nice person.'?" Philip asked.

"Well, there were rumors that he could be vicious and that he was a good person to stay away from." said Kevin.

"I heard that in an early grade he killed all the pet white rats in class. I have no proof of that, but that is what I heard. No one at school liked him but everyone was afraid of him."

"You said that he spoke to you at school; is that correct Kevin."

"Yes, but not for long; I think that he was just interested in me because I am an Indian. He wanted to know everything about me and my tribe. Once he learned what he wanted, he left me alone. I have not spoken to him in years."

Now Philip knew that he was on the right track. There was just too much coincidence regarding John. One, he was friends with Howard; two, his mother just died and he had no family and nothing holding him; three, the rumor was that he was nasty and may have killed animals in school. John had to be the second person in the car and Philip would bet his pension that John was the killer. Now he had to go to South Carolina to study the case.

"Detective, why are you interested in John?" asked Kevin.

"Even though it is not my case, I am interested in finding out who killed three people the night that Howard was killed."

"Three people?" said Kevin.

"Right; your friend Howard, a cop named Michael White and a lady named Suzy. The information that you just game me makes me very interested in your friend John."

"Detective, I hate to tell you this because I may be wrong but I am sure that I saw John with some changes to his face and he was driving an old car with a fresh paint job."

Now that made Philip interested in Kevin.

And it made Kevin interested in John. Where did John go? What became of him? Could it be possible that John was a murderer? Kevin knew that with John's history at school that anything was possible with John; and Kevin was glad that he never became a friend of John.

CHAPTER 21

Philip just could not get that triple murder and rape out of his mind. He didn't know if it was because a cop was killed or because a woman got raped. Because he had no life, he had lots of time after work to check the history of the crime and see what the other jurisdiction had turned up. Philip was so obsessed with the case that he decided to travel to South Carolina to check first hand with the local police department. He was very interested in this John person that Kevin mentioned. It was just very coincidental that John disappeared at the same time that the murders took place. Could John have been killed as well and the body disposed of or was John the killer? Based on the report that Officer Michael White called in on the stop, there were two people in the car; where was the other person? It seemed more and more likely that that other person was John and Philip wanted to catch him. The information that Kevin gave Philip led Philip to take a well-deserved early vacation and to try and discover everything that he could about this case. The real problem would be if the local police department would share this information. Since this case was several years old and was for all practical purposes a cold case, they should be willing to share, but you never know. Lots of small police departments don't like having big city police try to one up them. Philip decided to ask Kevin if he wanted to make the trip with him. Kevin would make good company and because of the information that Kevin had regarding John he might help with the investigation.

After calling the local police force Philip scheduled the trip for the following week for him and Kevin.

Kevin and Philip drove to a small town that was handling this case. and visited the local state trooper office where they were ushered in and introduced to trooper Moria White. Moria was five feet six inches tall and she looked like she knew her way around a gun and a grill. She was barely tall enough to be a trooper but she also looked like someone Philip did not want to tangle with. She made a good impression on Philip, even more so when he discovered that she was a fellow marine.

"Officer White, thank you for seeing us on short notice." said Philip.

"No problem; glad to help out a fellow cop and fellow marine." She said with a voice louder than her height would dictate. "How can I help you today?"

"I am interested in the triple murder that you had around here a few years ago. A police officer was killed as well as a passenger in a car and a woman who was raped and murdered and had her car stolen."

"Well, I certainly am familiar with that case. Anytime a police officer is killed that gets a lot of people interested."

"I know what you mean; I became interested for the same reason. I am also interested because we believe that the murdered car passenger was traveling with someone and that person has disappeared. That makes me wonder if he could have been involved or if he was also killed

CHAPTER 22

During the summer Kevin went back home to talk with his family and other members of the tribe. Once again, the Federal Government was breaking a treaty and a promise made by President John F. Kennedy. The Nation was told that a dam would not be built on the Allegheny River, but one was going to be built. This would not be some earthen dam but a monster that would be one of the largest dams in the Unites States east of the Mississippi River. Peter more than ever wanted to fight this construction before it was too late. Kevin did not get angry often but he was angry now. Once again, a document signed by government officials did not worth the paper it was written on.

PART 111
Weddings and Politics

CHAPTER 1

The wedding between Philip and Portia was a major social event. A five-piece band was there to help people move across the floor, and some of the best chiefs from the east coast were there to make whatever you wanted to eat, and fancy favors on each table. Anyone who was anyone was there. The women wore their best jewelry and the men all wore tuxedos. Even the mayor of Philadelphia was there as well as a ton of press photographers. Peter hoped that no one could recognize him from the photos in the paper. But someone did. Kevin saw the paper and his eyes opened wide because he was seeing someone from the past.

The wedding lasted till the early morning and most people were still there because the band was, smoking. Finally, when the clock struck 3, people slowly started to leave. Although the custom was for the bride and groom to leave early, Portia and Peter were the last to leave, not because Peter wanted to stay but because Portia was not in a hurry to join Peter. Peter of cause wanted to get to the wedding bed while Portia was not in any hurry to join Peter in his athletic moves. They were finally forced to leave because there were no more people there. Peter of course was hungry for his usual meal while Portia wished he went on a diet.

The next afternoon Peter and Portia were driven to the port in New York to catch a large fancy cruise ship. For the next three weeks they would cruise in comfit to many exotic locations with not much to do during the cruise but to eat fancy food and to fuck.

The cruise could not end soon enough for Portia. She felt that she needed a vacation to recover but she did have to start work and unknown to her Peter shot a silver bullet and she was pregnant.

CHAPTER 2

After the honeymoon Peter and Portia went to work, Portia for her father and Peter for a political organization.

Peter had started work in a political firm that was committed to getting democrats elected. Peter was a lawyer for the firm and it was his job to look for dirt, legally of cause, on the opposition. This was a perfect place for Peter to start his political career. It was a perfect place to make contacts with important people, people that were invited to his wedding, people that could get him elected

Working for the Democratic Election Committee was not back breaking work but was interesting to see how easy it can be to find information against your competitor. Everyone has secrets in the closet, some more than one. If you have good people at this job, they can find everything from sex secrets to fraud, to theft, to in Peters case, murder. Peter's history or lack of history is going to be a problem for Peter and the higher he goes in the political ladder the worse it will be. Peter thought about asking them to check him out, as a test, but then he decided that might be a bad idea, what if they did figure that he has a different name, then what. He would be shot down at the very beginning of his quest, better to hope that the ids that have worked so far would continue to work.

Portia worked as an executive, fitting her education and as the heir to the throne. She was very good at the job and no one resented her leadership position. Andrew could not be prouder than her. As a result of the vagina hurting cruise, she became pregnant with her first child, a girl.

The assets in Andrew's company continued to grow under Portia's leadership and so did Portia's stomach. Portia was happy to be pregnant because it made Andrew happy. Andrew always wanted a little granddaughter to pamper and he wanted to live long enough to give her what ever she wanted. Peter of course was only interested in work.

CHAPTER 3

Kevin contacted Philip as soon as he saw the picture in the local paper. The wedding was so big that it made even the local papers. Kevin and Philip made plans to meet at a diner midway between the two of them. The main issue to discuss was to see if they could prove that Peter was John, and was he the killer. If he was the killer, what could they do.

On the appointed day Kevin and Philip met at the well-known diner to discuss John. First of course they discussed how they were doing. Since they were both doing fine, they could skip to the real reason for this meeting. The first thing that they had to do was get DNA for both John and Peter. Kevin was positive that Peter was John, Philip was not so sure. Philip, as a cop, had many friends that could help. One thing that Philip recently found out was that two more people were killed by the same gun, that makes five. One was a plastic surgeon and the other was a well know crook who can get you whatever you wanted, like a plastic surgeon. When Kevin heard that, he became more positive that John changed his appearance and then had to kill the two people involved.

The gun that killed the three now five people had fingerprints on it, one set was one of the victims, the other was unknown. When the car was dusted, they had the same result. The real problem was getting Peter's prints. You just cannot go up to someone like him and ask for his prints; if you did and he was John then he would be suspicious. The only way to get the prints was in secret, pay someone to get them, and Philip knew just the person to do that.

CHAPTER 4

Working at his current job to elect democrats made it easy for Peter to have help running for office. The birth of his daughter, Sofia, made for a beautiful picture. Running for office, even just for state assembly was getting to be more work than Peter expected; but he had to start somewhere. Two terms of two years each should be enough to get him nominated for Governor. The current Governor, Jack "The Snake" Monroe, was sure to give up his seat by then and because of his age would not run again. That would make his job easy. Because of all the travel, Peter did not have much time with his wife and he was getting horny. He knew that it was dangerous to hook up with anyone while he was campaigning but he definitely had needs. He knew that there were women on the trail and in his campaign team that would be a "good fit," but could he chance it? He also had the problem of the campaign itself.

"How in the world do these idiot politicians do this every two years? It is driving me crazy. All the hands you must shake, the constant smiling, and the weird food you have to eat; it is beyond bizarre." thought Peter. But Peter knew that he had to do this or he would never get into office. He thought again about his needs and he made his mind up to wait until his wife joined him this weekend.

CHAPTER 5

"Why the flip is she still home; she knows how I need her." She was getting too uppity for Peter. She needed to be trained better and Peter would take care of that this weekend. After the great sex I will give her, he thought, she will do whatever I want. If someone else said that he would be bragging, but Peter was not. Peter was over confident in every thing he did, especially sex. He had many partners and they all went away satisfied. It was not just that he was big but that he knew what he was doing and what his partners wanted. Some wanted it slow and soft and others wanted it rough. Those were the types that he liked the best; the rougher the better. He especially liked the women that liked to be tied up and abused. There were not enough of those types to satisfy Peter but he could always hope. Unfortunately, his wife was only interested in a quickie and only in the missionary position. No matter how hard he tried (and he tried hard) she would not let him try anything else. It was almost as if she wanted to torment him. Even simple oral sex was out of the question for her. He even offered to use a condom but she still said no. Peter knew that he would need to find temporary partners once he got elected because his needs were not being satisfied. He would be very discrete of course, even if he had to pay a lot for it. There were certain places that were available for high priced politicians. They had the caliber women who knew how to satisfy and how to be quiet. He needed them to be both. He wondered if his wife knew about his partners. She probably had her suspicions but she never let on. She liked the good life as much as he did and she probably did not want to lose it any more than he did. Life at home and running for office was becoming boring to Peter and he did not like boring.

CHAPTER 6

Portia was beginning to have second and third thoughts about Peter running for office. She liked the lazy life she had before Peter began this crusade. He was a good lawyer and made good money; why did he need to be a politician? But she knew. Peter was one of those men that had to have power. She could tell by how he treated her. He always wanted to do things to her in bed and in other places but she would not allow it. She may have looked the part of an obedient wife but she knew what she was doing. She also knew that he found satisfaction elsewhere and she was good with that too; after all, she also wanted the power he could bring to her. Peter was too dumb to understand how she was playing him like a Stradivarius; and with luck, he never would hear how well she played.

Her father wanted her to take over the everyday running of the company and Portia knew that she could handle that responsibility but would she be able to be a head of a corporation and as the wife of a politician and a mother? The fact that she was a female CEO could help and hurt Peter's political career with some constituents and Portia was not sure what she should do. Part of her wanted the responsibility and part of her felt that she would see Peter even less than she did now. With Peter away she knew what he would be up to and it would not be with her. Portia was beginning to see why her father did not want her to marry Peter; but it was too late. There was no way the party would let her get a divorce. The party had big plans for Peter and they would not let her get in the way.

CHAPTER 7

Philip was becoming more interested in the triple now five-person murder case. He was not sure if it was because of the case or because of Moria. She could never replace Monica in Philip's life but he was having feelings for her. Moria was nothing at all like Monica. Moria was loud and rough while Monica was soft and feminine. Monica was light and romantic while Moria was robust. Philip was still young enough that he felt he could get involved again but every time he looked or talked to Moria all he could think about was Monica. He would remember the time that they had together and the joy that she gave him and he was afraid to try again. He kept arguing with himself over this because he knew that he was entitled to happiness again, but he was comfortable with his memory and his pain and that was the way it was going to be. He kept fighting with himself and every time he fought it wound up a draw.

CHAPTER 8

Kevin was still working at the large corporate firm, Cohen, Cohen, and Lawrence, that he started working for six months ago. He was doing well and making good money and as usual he was well liked by everyone at the firm. The problem was that Kevin wanted to make time to examine the treaty. This would mean fewer billable hours which would not make anyone at the firm happy. They knew from the beginning that Kevin was interested in pursuing this treaty but they hoped that he would lose interest and work hard for them. He did work hard for the firm but he never lost interest in the treaty. And then there was the issue with the now five murders. After the last talk with Philip, he was sure that John had surgery to change his appearance.

The last time that Kevin spoke to Philip they discussed how they were going about getting Peter's finger prints. Philip had friends that could get a cup or such as thing. It was easy to do with the right people and Philip had the right people.

CHAPTER 9

Peter won the election and was now a state representative. He had to work harder than he wanted to but less than he needed to in order to win the election.

The state capital was in Harrisburg and Peter needed to have a place to live when the chamber was in session. The place that Peter chose to use while in Harrisburg was a furnished two room apartment. It came with a small kitchen that had a table for eating and just enough to make coffee in the morning, because he had no reason to cook, he would eat out. Two bedrooms filled out the apartment.

Fitting his new position, he has two aids, one male, which did Peter no good, and one female which did. If he wins reelection, he would be entitled to another one. With any luck he will not need to run representative but for governor. He was already laying the ground work by getting tight with some of the longtime representatives and senators. He was also using the committee that he worked with, to see if they can find any dirt about the governor.

The House Chamber has 203 members, of which Peter would be one. The capital houses the legislative. chambers for the Pennsylvania General Assembly, made up of the Supreme and Superior Courts of Pennsylvania, as well as the officed of the Governor and the Lieutenant Governor It is also the main building of the Pennsylvania State Capital Complex. In order for Peter to go further than this position he needed to stand out. One way is to make friends with those representatives and Senators that have been there for a while. Those are the people that know how to get reelected. In general, they were also the ones that liked it where they were and did not want to go higher so, they were no competition to Peter. Another simple way to make Peter friends was to vote as the party wanted you to vote. The worse thing to do was vote the other party line. Peter was going to play it straight and vote the party line.

One of the good things about being in Hattiesburg was that he could check on the women and not have to worry about Portia. Portia was getting more and more unwilling to have the play time that Peter enjoyed. There was a member of his staff that liked the "bronco ride", a specialty that Peter invented. Harrisburg was not so bad after all.

CHAPTER 10

Portia was home a lot now that Peter was at the Capital. It was not easy to run a company and be a mother at the same time. Thank goodness her father loved baby sitting and playing with his new granddaughter. Portia's mother died three months after Portia gave birth, to her daughter Sofia her mother saw how beautiful her granddaughter was. Portia named her daughter Sofia after her mother. She was going to grow up to be like Portia and her mother. Peter wanted to name his daughter after his mother but he gave in to Portia. He figured that he could knock her up again.

Andrew was very happy playing with Sofia and he was just as happy with the job that Portia was doing running his firm. She learned a lot at Harvard about running a company and she made a few small changes that helped raise the profits for the firm by 15%. Portia needed to keep that from Peter because he might want to use the money to help run the next campaign. The Party might not fund the entire campaign because he was not important enough or had enough experience so Portia needed to protect her money from being used for Peter' next campaign. She knows that Peter wants to be Governor and he wanted money for that. If he wins reelection that means that he will try a higher spot.

CHAPTER 11

Peter needed to win the next election by a big number, which would make him more well known to the voters and the rest of the state that would be voting for governor Many people would be happy with two terms of governor of some state but Peter did not even want to serve one full term before he ran for president. That means that the powerbrokers, that make a president, need to see what Peter could do. That also means that Portia and Sofia needed to be seen more. That would require convincing Portia that being governor could not only help him but could help her company.

It took a lot of phone calls and eye to eye talks on the computer but they came to an agreement. Portia would go on trips, smile, and act like a good little wife and he would stop with the actions in bed that she could not tolerate. Peter only gave in because he knew he could get what he wanted from his staff and others. It was at this point that he only needed Portia to help him get elected. She was not useful for anything else.

CHAPTER 12

With Portia' absence Peter had to satisfy himself with a member of his staff, Daisy. She would do anything for Peter and anything he wanted she would do and he would do anything she wanted. She was a nice change from his cold wife. When he was campaigning, he would be sure to include Daisy on his travel staff. Because his term lasted two years, he had to campaign all the time, not only for the voters in his district but around the state. People needed to know who he was. He was trying to convince Portia that he could use her when he was campaigning but she always had an excuse. She was becoming useless in every way.

Peter's work at the capital was new and interesting. Getting laws passed was worse than seeing how sausage was made. Since his party held the house, it was easy to get any important law passed and Peter wanted his name on those bills as a supporter. When he was not working at the capital, he could see what games are played. He probably could not do anything about them but at least he listens, which is more than many other politicians do.

CHAPTER 13

Peter is becoming more well know. And the National Democratic leaders took notice. Because Peter was so handsome, many women and some men took notice as well. He was laying the ground work for his next climb up the ladder to run for governor. Also, with his constant campaigning he was rarely at home Thank God said Portia, let him stay out all the time Let someone else service Peter. With Peter gone she could continue working and playing with her daughter.

With all the campaigning that Peter did it was not a surprise that Peter won reelection. Now the next step, running for Governor. Because this was a state wide election he really needed his wife and daughter on the campaign for people to see. Governor was a four-year position but he was not going to wait that long. He was going to do things that will make people happy not only in his state but for other people in other states would like to have in their states would like to have in their state. He had to be careful because what might be popular in his state might not be popular in other states. In other words, he had to become a politician.

As a two-term state representative he had a bigger office and a bigger staff. He kept Daisy on his staff because he wants to keep her close. He still had to work at his regular job in the capital but he also had to lay the ground work for the next election. He did his best to get close to the leaders, those who were in politics for a long time. He would talk to those who could help him get to the next level. Most of them thought that he meant the senate but he meant the Governor.

Peter stayed in the capital most of the time working with senior members in the house and senate letting them know who he was and helping them when he could. He is going to need a lot of help to make the next move.

CHAPTER 14

Because of all the hard work that Peter did working with leaders in the capital, he was able to convince them to pick him as the party candidate for Governor. There were several people with more experience including an attractive woman business leader who would make a nice Governor but Peter's hard work paid off. The leaders picked him,

Campaigning had started for Governor and the competition was weaker than Peter expected. The Republican candidate was not well known in the state and having no experience in politics had no backing, He was a rich CEO of a mid-size company so he had money but would he spend it. Peter was able to convinced Portia to join him to some of the unreliable Republican areas in the hope to get some of the voters who were on the fence. The Republican party was spending because Pennsylvania does not always swing there way.

Portia was not happy traveling to the places she had to go, nor was she happy shaking hands with so many people, and eating strange food all the time. What she would not do foe a nice salad. She had to do these things to keep Peter happy and to keep him off her back, so to speak. Portia gave in to Peter regarding her travel with him but, she held the line for Sofia. Her daughter was not going to travel but she would stay home with a loving grandfather. Because both of them were tired, they did not have the energy for extra special activities.

The campaign could not end soon enough for both Peter and Portia. She could not wait to **be** home with Sofia, who was growing up before her eyes.

CHAPTER 15

The campaigning was over and the votes were in. Somehow the other party was able to get more money for campaigning and made the outcome close. Peter did win but with a smaller margin then expected. This was not good for Peter because it made him look weak to the leaders in the party. He was going to have to work hard in the presidential primaries.

For the time being he would be the top executive in Pennsylvania a major eastern state. The Governor has a lot of branches that reported to him such as police and transportation.

Governor was an important political position because there were only fifty of them and sometimes, they would meet as a group in Washington.

Peter had one of the best staff money could buy and it did cost. When Peter throws his hat in the ring to run in the presidential primaries in three years, he hopes that the party would give some money for the primaries but they probably will feal that there was a stronger candidate and that is the horse they wanted to ride into Washington. Governors seemed to have a lot of power but the real power is only in their state. Peter was happy to be a Governor but he had other ideas.

CHAPTER 16

Peter was now settled in the capital. The large apartment reserved for the governor was well furnished but empty because Portia refused to leave home. She wanted to continued with her job and she likes being where she can play with her daughter and how happy she is when she has her father playing with Sofia. She had no reason to move. Although Peter wanted her there, in the capital, he knew that he could not satisfy her so he did not argue with her about moving to the capital. That did not look like a happy family to many people including the leaders in Washington but he used the excuse that she was running a medium size company while also being a mother. That seemed to work and made enough sense to keep the leaders quiet. Peter still had Daisy but there was a limit on how many times he could sneak her into his room. Peter needs to find a way to get Portia to come visit for at least a weekend.

CHAPTER 17

Kevin and Philip did not meet often but did talk on the phone regarding the John/Peter issue. They saw the pictures of the new Governor and both had to agree that Peter did look like John after slight plastics surgery. The fact that a probable murder could get to be governor seemed imposable and it would take a lot of evidence to prove. Several times in political history governors lost their job because of indiscretion but not for murder. The press would go wild and the impact on the party would reverberate for several elections. Finger print match would not be enough they also need a DNA match and that might not be enough to prove that John was Peter.

CHAPTER 18

Being Governor was a prestigious job. There were only fifty Governors and each of them controlled everything in a state. That state could be small like Delaware or large like Alaska. Each state had thousands or sometimes millions of people trying to live with piece in their life. Those people counted on the politicians in the state to keep them safe among other things and if Peter wanted to be President, he needed to be a great Governor and show the political leaders what he could do as President.

Portia of course lived most of the time at home with her job, her father, and her beautiful daughter. Peter wanted her with him so they could play games and maybe make another baby. Two babies would look good on the campaign trail; it would make him look viral.

Peter has never worked this hard even when he campaigned for his first election. He needed to be on tv as much as possible He needed to be like senator Summer who is on tv every Sunday. As far his play time he has to "lay off" Daisy for a while, people were starting to get the right idea about her real duties.

CHAPTER 19

Peter worked hard for the people of his state and he did some good things for them. Besides working for his constituents, he also traveled to many important primary states. Some state primaries were going to be tough to win but if he came in second, he would still get some primary votes. He was in a hurry to become President so he had to work harder than before to be nominated. In this case there were going to be 14 candidates running for president so Peter felt his best change was to knock off as many as he could with bad knowledge about the candidates. His team would have to work hard again.

CHAPTER 20

Two years of working as governor did not exactly fly by but it was better than he expected. He loved the power that he had and he actually liked getting things done. Primary session would be starting soon and he needed to get in the running in the beginning. As Peter guessed, the party wanted someone with more experience and money and Morrow had both. Peter would have to do as much as he could to change the party leader's mind. One thing that he could do quietly was to have his team check out the other candidates for any that could be knocked out of competition.

It was easy to find information on five people running, they did not have really bad marks on their job history, just enough to have them leave the race. That left nine to go. Two dropped off because they did not have enough support and three more left because they ran out of money that left four, the cream of the crop which included Peter.

Peter was working hard on the small states because they were not in Morrow's pocket. Peter's people show that there was a high percent of undecided and he wanted them. Rumer has it that Peter was in second place with the important people. Morrow was still on top and it looked like he intended to stay there. One more candidate dropped which left just three. One other candidate looked like he was running out of money and was sure to drop out, this would leave Morrow and Peter to fight it out. Peter was trying to take the dropout's votes away from them but they were playing hard to get because Morrow was doing the same thing. Morrow was offering key positions for the votes while Peter could not offer the same. That's how it works, turn your votes over to another candidate and when he wins, he will give you a low-level cabinet job. Peter did not have the power to do that.

CHAPTER 21

It was becoming obvious to Peter that he probably would not win the nomination for President. The party leaders were concerned that he did not have the experience or enough money to run a successful campaign. Peter was not sure how much more experience he needed but he knew that he was not going to wait another four or eight years to run a primary campaign again. Once is more than enough, he thought. As for the money; they were right. He could not raise as much money as Jason Paul Morrow, Senator from Florida, but nobody could. Morrow had the unions and the best money man in Washington on his side. Because of Morrow's premature aging he had white hair and that made him attractive to the elderly and it also gave the impression that he was experienced. There was no doubt that he would carry Florida, a big get state that both parties courted. Peter could not compete with Jason. His only hope was the second spot on the ticket, a position that was becoming more likely as the campaign continued.

There was a rumor that Morrow was debating who he wanted for his vice-president and Peter was on the short list. Peter needed a way to get to the top of that list. This was the year that his party would finally regain the white house and Peter wanted to be part of that. Once there he could work on climbing that last step. Peter was debating his options. What could he do that would make Jason pick him? Peter thought about that while his staff babbled on about things that were of no concern of his. Peter knew that if his wife was more accommodating and willing that she could probably convince Jason to pick Peter. But that would never happen. She was too "normal" to bend over or make like an Electrolux to help Peter. This left other options. The most obvious was; Peter could help Jason with the election.

Jason was not a bad public speaker, but he was not in Peter's class.

Peter also had better appeal with the women voters. Peter also had executive experience as a governor. All these reasons made Peter a good choice for vice-president but some of the other candidates also had good qualifications. Peter's biggest competition was Charles Burger. Charles was a popular two term governor of a Midwest state and was friends with Jason. This was a dangerous combination for Peter. Peter needed some way to discredit Charles and that is what he was going to do. Peter had people on his payroll that could dig up dirt on Mother Theresa. The best dirt involved an affair, or love child, or even better, a same sex relationship. What was that phrase that he heard, "Don't get caught in bed with a dead girl or a live boy?" Lots of people could be bought if the money was high enough, and it would be for the right information. Not paying taxes would not work because most politicians 'forget" to pay taxes but stealing that was another matter. Peter also had to worry about anyone finding dirt about him, but since his identity change, he had been a reasonably good boy. It was his life as John that would get him in trouble if someone could connect the dots. He was sure that he did not leave a trail behind, but he could not be sure. And not being sure was troubling.

The first item on his agenda for today was to get his people to search for information on Charles. That had already started during the campaign but now it would go in full swing. Everyone had skeletons in their closets and he would find Charles's. Next would be his wife, she was still the best-looking spouse of the VP candidates and she knew it. She needed to get front and center so more people would see her but she also needed to not speak. Peter did not need her to cause him trouble by saying something inappropriate. What was that saying, "Remain silent and be thought a fool, speak and remove all doubt?" She would remove all doubt. Even after all these years Peter did not understand how very smart Portia was and how useful she could be if he let her. To Peter she was just a dumb blonde who was not very good in bed; but she was neither. She was smarter than him and could be better in bed if she was not repulsed by Peter.

117

Peter and his investigating staff met after lunch and discussed a multiple-way search for incriminating data on Charles.

"Jack, you need to spearhead this investigation and it must be legit and quick. I don't want anyone to say that we planted dirt on Charles." said Peter.

"Understood Governor; anything that we find will be real."

"Be creative Jack. We have some initial dirt from the primaries so that would be a good starting point. Maybe something will turn up from one of those stories."

Jack Howard was an aid that had been with Peter for years and he understood Peter the way no one else did. He also would do anything for Peter and the combination of knowledge and loyalty made jack a dangerous person for Peter; someone to handle with kid gloves.

And as usual with Jack working the plan, something did turn up; something that not only would knock Charles out of contention, but drive him from politics as well. Charles had a long-time boyfriend. The boy friend was well hidden and no one, not even on his staff, knew about Christian. Christian was a young, tall, thin, blond who liked rough sex. And Charles was happy to oblige. They had been together since Christian was fifteen and Charles kept Christian happy with a nice apartment with all the trimmings. This was more than a home run for Peter. Not only was Charles having sex with a boy but it was a young boy and it was rough sex. Funny how good things happy to bad people like Peter.

Peter now needed to get this information out to the press. He also needed proof, such as pictures and tapes. He had someone very good who could be counted on to take the pictures and make the audio tapes and that would be first on todays to do list.

CHAPTER 22

As Peter expected the press went crazy when the pictures and audio of Christian and Charles Burger were released. People could not believe that a person of Charles stature and political experience could be involved with a young boy for years and no one knew. This would do wonders for his career, not to mention his life at home. People were wondering what his wife would do and how his children would take the news. People in the news industry were salivating because everyone knew that Charles was going to be picked as the vice-presidential candidate. People also wondered what impact this would do for the candidacy of Senator Morrow. Morrow needed to hit a home run with whomever he picked to run with him or he was sure to lose the election.

Morrow's team also knew they needed to hit a home run or at least a triple. The team was lucky that they had not introduced Charles as the vice-presidential candidate yet; therefore, they could deny that he would have been picked.

CHAPTER 23

The nominating convention was being held in Detroit this year, for no good reason other than the party wanted to appeal to the poor. As if the party cared for the poor; they just wanted their votes. Detroit was also a Democratic city so that also helped with the voters.

Nominating Conventions were a zoo. People holding up signs for their candidate, every one yelling, smoking in back rooms, and more. There was not much suspense because Morrow had the votes but it still was exciting. Because of the issue with Charles as the vice-presidential candidate Morrow had no choice but to select Peter as his running mate and he was already running and campaign for the party. He also campaigned with other candidates in the same state. The more state and federal candidates who win would make it easy to get bills passed. Morrow and the democratic leaders have taken notice how hard Peter is working for the party and they were happy that he was available to be the new VP.

CHAPTER 24

The day before Election Day was more hectic than any other days in Peter's memory. The polls indicated that it was a close race and one state would make the difference in the election. Jason Paul Morrow had people working overtime to get out the vote in Florida; although as a two-term senator from Florida it would be unbelievable how he could lose that state. Peter had people working in Pennsylvania and some of the smaller states that were still up for grabs because every state was still in play. This would be the closest election that anyone could remember. That's what you get when you have two good candidates running; the independents were the difference. Peter was spending Portia's money to get out the vote and she would definitely expect payment. Peter was not worried about that but he was worried about losing. If he lost, he would need to go thought this again but this time at the top of the ticket. This left him with the thought, "Would it be better to lose and run again in four years, or win and figure out how to kill the president?" That was an interesting question and Peter was not sure of the answer. Losing would make it easy because he had the organization ready and he would surely be nominated the next time, plus he did not have to kill again. But as usual Peter could not wait; he wanted everything now. No, Philip wanted to win now and take his chances. He would find a way, he always did.

All the polls on the East coast were already closed and the results were beginning to come in as expected. The other side was winning where they were expected to win and Peter's side was taking some of the other states. Florida was still up for grabs as was Georgia, two large electoral states. The mid-west polls would be closing soon with the only state this year

sure to be on the other side was Illinois. Normally Illinois would be in Peter's pocket but this year the Republican candidate was the Illinois governor who was very popular. The big test would be California and Texas;

they would be the final piece of the puzzle and even though California usually goes one way and Texas goes the other it was anyone's guess as to how they would go.

The TV pundits were all going crazy because of the excitement of the election and many of the correspondents said that it would be a long night and that the results may take another day for them to call a victor. But they were wrong; it would take a week before the results and recounts were in. And election night became the week of hell for the nation.

CHAPTER 25

Finally, after all the recounts the nation knew who the president would be. Morrow pulled it out by a slim amount. And that was because of the state of Arizona which normally goes Republican since Goldwater this time went Democrat by less than 70,000 votes. Arizona was one of the medium size states that Peter worked hard to swing them to Democratic and Morrow would not forget that. For a week the newspapers and TVs had nothing except voting information as the votes swung back and forth before the winner was named. Peter was going to be the Vice President of the United States.

Peter could not believe it and neither could Portia; but the people who really could not believe it were Kevin and Philip. Now it looked like the Vice President of the United States was a murder. Philip and Kevin discussing for hours what they should do and they would continue to discuss the issue the next day. Something had to be done, they could not let Peter become the VP.

CHAPTER 26

━┿━ ❁ ━┿━

Peter was so bored that he has taken to reading poetry. Now he understands when someone once said being vice President was like a bucket of spit. There was no way that he could do this for four or God forbid eight years. It is not easy for a vice President to become president. Voters seem to think that a Vice President becoming president is just a continuation of the president's term and they usually want a change. Peter had to come up with a way to get rid of the president without incriminating himself. There are just too many secret services people around him all the time. And then Peter had an idea. After he gets swoon in, he will work on the plan.

CHAPTER 27

Portia liked being the wife of the vice-president and she still enjoyed the sex, but she was tired of the way Peter treated her in private. The only thing she was to Peter was an ornament and a group of body parts. She knew that one day Peter would be President but Portia did not know how much more she could tolerate. She was well aware of his discretions and had been for some time. Portia had heard that Peter was cheating on her when they were dating and after they were married. Portia did not mind because she had her fun as well but it still made her angry. Her fun was in frustrating Peter because unlike Peter she was monogamous; and she was beginning to be bored with being monogamous. That was one of the reasons why she held out on him. Peter wanted to have sex all different ways and she would have gladly complied but because of his arrogance she refused. She was never sure if that was one of the reasons why Peter cheated, could he be getting what he wanted somewhere else? It did not matter because sex wasn't as important to her as it obviously was to Peter. She was giving serious consideration to a divorce but that would never happen. The party would never let her divorce because that would screw up the family picture. Somehow, she would figure out how to end the abuse.

CHAPTER 28

The White House was huge and Peter loved it when he had to visit. He knew that one day he would be the one living there instead of at the Vice-presidential house, called Number One Observatory Circle, which was barely as large as Portia's family home. It was a three-story brick house with a little over 9,000 square feet of floor space. The house's first floor has a dining room, garden room, living room, lounges, pantry kitchen, reception hall, sitting room, and veranda. The second floor contains the main bedroom suite, an additional bedroom, a den, and a study. The attic, once the servants' quarters, now houses four bedrooms. The main kitchen is located in the basement. As the vice-president he has security around the clock and at his new home and when he went out for his secret rendezvous,

PART IV

Succession

CHAPTER 1

The day of the inauguration turned out to be cloudy and cold. Peter did not care because he had just been sworn in as the Vice President of the United States. His mother would be so proud and when he becomes president, she would have been even prouder. President Morrow gave a nice speech, not as good as Kennedy's but better than most. As Vice President Peter did not need to give a speech all he had to do was say the oath, which he did perfectly.

Tonight, there would be many parties with "fat cats" who would be invited to meet the new administration. Each of them asking what we could do for them. This is definably the land of "what can you do for me."

Portia looked fabulous in her beaded Armani gown; she was definitely the best looking and the best dressed woman at the inauguration ball; but then she always was the best looking and best dressed no matter where she went. Peter wore a 100% cashmere Armani tuxedo and looked fabulous, if he did say so himself. Peter did not realize that every man looked great in a tux. Peter Marks, Vice President, had such a great ring to it that Peter could get used to hearing it; but not for long; he had bigger fish to fry. He would do what ever it took to get to the top and since he could not wait for that to happen that included killing the President. Several presidents have been assassinated and there were attempts on the lives of at least three others, what is one more. Peter had to plan this carefully and leave no doubt that he was not involved; but how? The President was under constant secret service watch, as was Peter; how in the world can he pull this off? He did not come this far to settle for second prize. But tonight was not the night for such thoughts; tonight was the night to enjoy everything that he had accomplished. How Peter wished that his mother could see him now; a poor kid from Pennsylvania made it to become Vice President. He would satisfy his hunger for Portia tonight; and she better not hold out on him tonight of all nights.

There were multiple balls to attend tonight and then the work of the administration would start. President Morrow had several big ideas on his agenda and with the presidency and a slight majority of congress in the same hands he had a good chance of keeping some campaign promises. As VP Peter oversaw NASA, this was a long-time job requirement that he knew nothing about. Peter would just be another member at the president's meetings and he was just another voice that the President probably would not listen to; but Peter would sit and be quiet and learn and bide his time until he could make his move. And he would make his move because he was in too much of a hurry to wait his turn. He read somewhere that the best presidents were those that ran because they knew that it was their turn to be president; and he believed it. He did not care if he was the best president; he just wanted to be president.

When Peter and Portia finally made it to the VP's house the first place that Peter went was to the bedroom and the last place that Portia wanted to go was the bedroom. After all the parties Peter took out his joy and appetite on Portia. As usual Portia resisted some of the more unusual methods that Peter really enjoyed. This made both angry. Peter knew that he had to look elsewhere for his usual sex games. He found it with his usual aid, Daisy and both were happy.

CHAPTER 2

Kevin had known for some time that Peter Marks was John but what could he do about it? He contacted his friend Philip but Philip had known that he could not just go up to the Vice-President of the United States and accuse him of being a murderer. What if he was wrong? What if Kevin was wrong? They both had to have evidence but whatever evidence they could find would be too old and useless to be of any use.

They had the fingerprints on the gun but not any DNA. Philip had a friend that worked at the White House and he might be able to get a cup with Peter's fingerprints and DNA but it would require questions. An easy answer would be that Philip always wanted a souvenir that the VP used. Lots of people had souvenir from the President but not from the VP. That was weak but it should work, and it did. The cup with the fingerprints and DNA was sent out and now all they had to do was wait.

The DNA test was taking a long time and he doubted that they would be useful. The sperm from Suzy had been saved and preserved but would they be useable after all these years? But then the results came in.

Philip looked at the results again and again and still he could not believe what he was seeing.

"My God," he said, "John Water is Peter Mark, the Vice President. Holy crap, that cannot be true."

But it was. Philip had to sit down and read the results again. John Water, a man who murdered at least five people was really Peter Mark the current Vice President of the United States. How in the world could that be? And what does he do about it? Philip had to sit down and think over his options. He could notify the FBI with the information that he has. He could try to arrest him himself. He could work with Kevin and see what he thinks. No matter what, this was too big for him to decide.

Philip was beginning to enjoy talking to Kevin. These conversations gave him something to do and to take his mind off Monica. Life was not as good as it would be if he were still married, in fact he would not be in Erie if he were still married. Philip was enjoying Kevin and he was beginning to think of him as a friend; and Philip desperately needed a friend. The other cops enjoyed working with Philip but they did not hang out together. Philip was too quiet and bleak. Most of the other cops were on their second marriage and social activities did not usually include single people. Some of the cops and their wives tried to fix Philip up with a friend or neighbor, but Philip always said no. That left Philip alone after work and that's how he liked it until he met Kevin. Philip was not sure what life had in store for Kevin, but he knew that Kevin would excel in whatever he chose to do.

There was a friend that Philip met when he went to FBI school for some specialist training, maybe he could help. It was some time ago that he took the class but Philip remembered how professional the instructor was. He believed that he had an Irish name, Patrick he believed.

CHAPTER 3

Patrick O'Connor was a US Secret Service agent and he was very good at his job. He started working for the government in the FBI, which was almost as hard to get into as the secret service, and now he was working protection detail for the President of the United States. As far as Patrick was concerned, this was the best job in the world. The only thing that Patrick liked better was his family. It was unusual for a family man to be on protection duty because they worked long hours that often-involved foreign travel. Patrick was the exception. He was on protection detail because of his skill and dedication; he *would* take a bullet for the president. He had already proved how good he was when a crazed teen tried to stab the previous president. It happened one rainy night in Baltimore, where the president had gone to make a speech. The president was shaking hands and between the rain, the darkness and the umbrella covering the president it was hard to see the seven-inch knife that an eighteen-year-old high school teenager; angry at the world, himself, or just angry, thrust at the president. Patrick saw the glint and placed himself between the knife and the president and as a result Patrick took the knife in the lower ribs. He received a medal for his actions as well as a nice scar but what he really was happy for was the praise from other members of the detail. They knew a professional when they saw one.

Patrick was married for ten years and he and his wife had two beautiful children. They had to be beautiful because his wife, Marge, was the most beautiful woman he had ever seen. Even though Patrick was a good-looking man he still every day thanked the heavens that they looked like her and not him. Marge could have been a professional model or a high earning movie star but because of her interest in physics she went to college, took all the science classes, and came out of college as a science teacher. Patrick met Marge in a college physics class; which still strikes Patrick as funny; a beautiful woman taking physics. Patrick was "hit by a thunder bolt" when he first saw Marge and he knew that he had a chance because of the way that Marge smiled at him. They dated for two years before Patrick was able to persuade Marge to marry him. He did not need any persuasion.

Marge was no prude but she did make Patrick wait for their first sexual encounter and Patrick was both relieved and glad for the wait. She was more than he wanted and he was afraid that he could not satisfy her and therefore he might lose her. No chance. Marge loved him as much as he loved her. He was without a doubt the strongest man Marge had ever seen but he was gentle and kind. He had a great smile and loved children and she knew that he would be a good husband to her and any children they might have. She did not have to wait long to find out because she became pregnant on their honeymoon; it must have been luck she thought to herself. Their first child was a son

CHAPTER 4

Peter gave a lot of thought to how to kill the President. The President had so many security people that it would impossible to get close to him. Of course, Peter could get close but that was ridiculous because then he would be shot down in a minute. He could have a secret agent do it but that would require a big bribe such as kidnapping his family but that would be difficult because many of the agents because of the work they do rarely have a family. There may be other ways but they all needed extra people and that goes against his motto, "You need to do the crime by yourself so that were no witnesses." And then Peter had an idea. The President took a daily pill for his heart. Most people did not know that. He did not take the pill alone but an agent was in the room with him to be sure that he took the pill. Peter had an idea. If he could put some medicine that could be harmful to his heart in his capsule that would do the trick. The question now was how to get the other medicine.

There was someone on Peter's staff who had a major hot for him. It was easier to have a "guest" as VP then before when he was a representative and their quality now was better. They had experience and knew when necessary and knew to keep their mouth closed but also when to keep it wide open. Daisy was her name and she would do anything for Peter, and she always did, and he would do anything to her, and he always did. She was with Peter since he was a representative. Since she was still on his staff, she could visit Peter and he could use the Presidents bathroom and put the new pills in the jar. One day he would take the "right" pill and cheers to the new president.

Peter came up with another method, a sleeping pill crushed up and added to his capsule would do the trick. Since Morrow took his medicine at night, he would fall asleep and die in his sleep. It would look like a normal death from his heart problem. All he needed was to ask Daisy to get him two of her pills. He used the excuse that he was having trouble sleeping because of all the pressure. And so, the plan took effect. Peter got the pills and put some of the powder in the two of the capsules. Now all he had to do was wait.

CHAPTER 5

For some reason the President called Peter into the Oval Office for a "talk." Peter could not remember the last time that this happened. The Oval Office is the room for important meetings and talks. When Peter arrived, he was offered a chair. Since it was just the two of them so he had his choice pf comfortable chairs; then the President started to speak.

"Peter, do you have any ideas of running for President"?

When Peter heard that he did not know whether to be afraid or jump for joy. Jumping for joy would not be presidential so he just said: "What do you mean"?

"Peter, do you expect to run for higher office?"

"Well, that's a long time to go. "You have 4 or 7 years left."

"Peter, do you know that I take heart pills every day?"

"Yes of course but that is not really common knowledge."

"My cartologist does not believe that they are doing a good job anymore and the top heart specialist check me out and she agrees. They believe that the pressure of the job is causing the problem and they believe if I do not resign, I will not last the year. Tomorrow at 9pm on national tv I will resign and you will be sworn in as the new President. Congratulations."

Peter almost had his own heart attack with that news. He would be President and he did not have to kill anyone to get the job. Portia was really going to suffer tonight. No way she is going to say no to her husband and the President. It was about time that she learned who was in charge.

"Peter, I would suggest that you do not make many changes to the staff. We have good people that know their job and they can help you a lot. If you want, I will stay on a week to help you get familiar with things, you did not attend many important meetings and that was my fault so I want to help you catch up on things. I hope that you will continue the path I was on because it is a good program."

"I know many of your staff because I helped pick them out. I think that the first thing to do is have a meeting with the senior staff and then a meeting with several lower-level staff. I would love to have your assistance. You were good enough to pick me for the picket so I want to continue your plan as best I can. I am not sure how this will impact the next election because you were more popular than me."

"Peter, If I am still alive, I will work with the party to get good party people elected." I guess that is all for now. Go home and tell your wife the news. She will make a beautiful first lady."

Yes, she will be thought Peter especially now that she has a bun in the oven.

CHAPTER 6

When Peter arrived home, after his meeting with the President, he was all smiles. Portia thought that maybe he had an afternoon delight. Good, then he will leave me alone. But he did not. After a quick dinner of macaroni and bolognaise sauce Peter dragged Portia into the bedroom but Portia would not have any of that. Portia fought back until Peter gave her a smack on her perfect check. Portia did not cry she just fought back harder. This caused Peter to toss her on the bed and tie her up with rope that he had prepared for such an event. Portia fought back even harder but she was no match for Peter.

Now that she was secure Peter abused her every way his sick mind could think of. Every place he could put his gorged piece he did. Portia tried to scream but she had been gaged. When he was finished, he finally untied her and removed the gag. He was exhausted and felt that Poria got the message; that he was the one in charge and she better get with the program but, all it did was make her angrier than she ever was and no matter what the party wanted she would get rid of Peter; one way or another.

CHAPTER 7

Peter got up early, took a shower, and dressed with one of his Amani suits. Later he would change into a more formal suit for the changing of the guard before a huge TV audience. He could not believe how easy it was to become President. What made it easier was that Peter had not put the new pills in the jar yet so there was nothing to remove. Life has really become great; all his dreams have come true.

CHAPTER 8

Philip caught up to Kevin at the gate and both were met by Patrick. Philip and Kevin were setup to talk to Patrick in one of the White House private rooms, to discuss the VP issue. Philip brought all the reports and information that they would need to decide what to do. After Patrick gave a quick review of the documents, especially the DNA report and he felt that he needed to tell his boss. He also had a feeling that the President might be in jeopardy because of the meeting he had last night and the TV show set up for tonight. Something is going on. First things that he needed to do was make sure that the President was protected more than usual. He would personally take security watch over the VP just to be sure. In addition, Portia decided to visit her husband today, Patrick knew about the abuse she takes so maybe she has decided to live at her regular home and leave Peter to the well-known secret that everyone knew about Daisy. What else could go wrong today.

CHAPTER 9

Bill was one of the youngest secret service agents on presidential detail. He joined the secret service right after graduate school and extensive FBI training, not because he wanted to protect the president, but because he liked to travel. So far, he was not doing as much travel as he expected. President Jason Paul Morrow was not as active as some previous presidents and he liked to spend his down time at Camp David. Bill's real name was Bill Club and he could never live it down. He would be made fun of at school but especially when he joined the service.

"Hey Billy, bring your club" or

"Here comes the Billy Club"; were just two of the better responses he would hear.

That did not bother Bill, he loved what he was doing and he intended to do it until he was too old to run beside the presidential car. That assignment was usually reserved for the younger agents. When the president was home in DC Billy had duty in the White House. He had to make sure the President was safe; as if anyone could get in this building.

CHAPTER 10

There was a lot of action this morning. Patrick and Billy went to guard the VP from doing anything to the VP. Patrick's boss would be over later to read the documents and he would add extra security for the VP if necessary. Extra security for the Presentation was also scheduled and he would contact his boss if it appeared necessary. What Patrick told him and the documents say would give Patrick's boss chills as it did to him.

Philip and Kevin both went as extra pairs of eyes to protect the President. No one was watching Portia as she entered Peter's office. Very calmly she removed her father's gift and put two bullets in Peter's chest and one in Peter's favorite organ.

Portia was not able to take it anymore. Peter just would not abide by the simple rule of marriage, monogamy. Even as Vice-President he still could not keep his wick dry.

Portia could not believe the sound of the gun. It and the kick were much louder than she expected. If she was not holding the gun so hard the bullets could have gone anywhere; but it went where it was supposed to go; at Peter.

Billy and Patrick both saw the glint of the gun and heard the noise as well as the other people near by They all came running to try to stop what was happing but Billy was first and he jumped on Portia to prevent any more damage to Peter, but it was too late.

Peter thought that he was still conscious and he was sure that he could see his mother looking down at him. She was dressed in light and was more beautiful than he could remember. She looked like she must have looked when she was young and well. She looked disappointed but Peter could not tell why; was she disappointed because Peter was shot? When Peter looked at his mother again, she looked so far away, like she was rising or he was falling or perhaps both. When Peter looked at his mother again, she was too far away to see and then all Peter could see was darkness, darkness darker than the darkest night, darker than the absence of all light, darkness that surrounded him and would not let him go.

EPILOG

Because of Peter's logs and notes and the many women that came forward to verify the writings. and also, easy to verify data that Peter was John and he murdered six people. The notes identified the young girl, that he murdered when he was seven proving that he was an eviler person then original thought.

Portia was tried for murder but no one wanted to find her guilty. When her defense told the jury and the large tv audience what she went through dealing with Peter and because she saved the President's life they came to a quick verdict of not guilty. Portia still works as the CEO of her father' firm. Both her and her father love to play with her daughter and both hoped that she would grow up to be a normal girl and woman and not sick like her father. Portia never remarried. She had enough of men.

Because of the beating that she received from Peter, she lost her baby, a boy. In a way she was glad that she lost the baby. She was afraid the child would be molded by Peter in to someone like himself.

Kevin left his corporate job and now lives and works at the reservation. He met a nice tribal woman, also a lawyer, and the two of them are still working on the treaty and other Indian affairs and on their upcoming wedding.

Philip is now a senior detective but still alone. He thinks of Monica every day and cannot see any one that can replace her.

Daisy was fired for unauthorized relations with a superior. She was not charged with any thing else because she did not talk about the sleeping pills.

Patrick received his second medal for helping to save the President's life. He also received a promotion that allowed him to work in DC and left him to stay home with his family and his pregnant wife.

Billy Club was given a medal for jumping on Portia and for trying to save the VP. No one makes jokes about his name anymore. Because of all the issues with the Morrow administration, Morrow was never reelected. Peter never got to be President but the Speaker of the House did.

Printed in the United States
by Baker & Taylor Publisher Services